MUSICAL VOYAGE

Nelly Venselaar

iUniverse, Inc.
New York Bloomington

Musical Voyage

iUniverse books may be ordered through booksellers or by contacting:

iUniverse
1663 Liberty Drive
Bloomington, IN 47403
www.iuniverse.com
1-800-Authors (1-800-288-4677)

ISBN: 978-1-4401-7949-5 (pbk)
ISBN: 978-1-4401-7950-1 (ebk)

Printed in the United States of America

iUniverse rev. date: 10/7/2009

Acknowledgements

Many, many thanks to our daughter Eveline, who spent numerous hours and telephone calls editing this book. I am grateful for the encouragements of Harry and Yvonne and the patience and help of our middle daughter Dr. Marie Anne Mundy, who helped me through many computer crises.

Family Tree

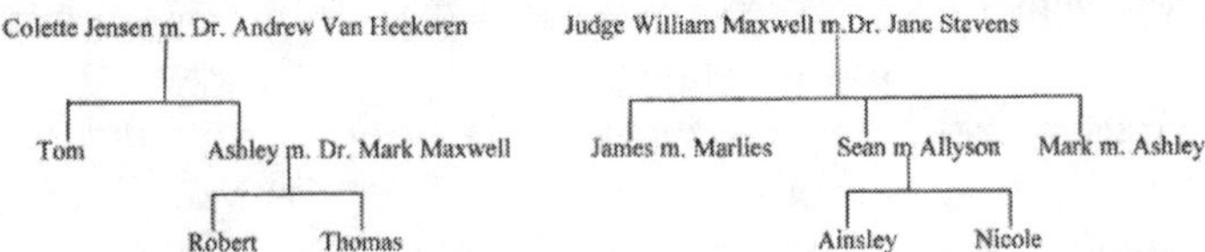

Peter Thompson friend of Andrew Van Heekeren m. Marion
Jim Walker, concertmaster and friend of Mark
Ken Ashton, conductor
Caroline Bromley- Illustrator
Dr. Thornton, Dean of Music Department
Lisa, piano student
Dr. Campbell, President of University of B.C.
Dr. Whittaker, Prof. at the Architecture Department
Prof. Maurice St. Denis m. Lucille, Montreal University
Minah, Colette's help
Asha and Asita , Ashley's helpers- students

MUSICAL VOYAGE

The sound of violin music forms a balance between music and nature.
Enchanting illusions, velvety, husky passionate tones inspire us.
Moods of the violin may send us visions of mountains in the clouds.
Variation of rhythm, tone, voice, as well as
Flow of music may change into dreamy melodies.

The orchestra alters the mood, showing other visions.
What's more beautiful and moving than seeing hills
And valleys through a soft mist?
Music offers a translation of a heavenly painting.

Pipe dreams and castles in the air envisioned
Willows overhanging the softly flowing river,
Bach's Air or the Peer Gynt may show grapes growing in the sunshine,
This music muse carries us away and makes us ponder about life.

Fairy-tale landscapes with sunflowers
Or pinky-orangey clouds at sunset appear.
What is the hidden meaning of a fugue?
Is there idealistic striving of the unconscious?

A shepherd visualizing his flock of sheep in a beautiful valley,
Soaring swallows against the blue sky,
Likening nature to emotional violin music

All this harmony in music carries nature's truth;
Making us aware of delightful, serene vistas.

Violin music is like a prayer
Offering peace and beautiful thoughts;

Saturating mankind with artistic musings.

Nelly Venselaar
2006

CHAPTER 1

After a dangerous and more than exciting crossing of the North Sea from Holland, Colette and her parents arrived in Tilbury, England.

They had escaped from the Nazis!!

The Germans had invaded the Netherlands and their planes were bombing the city of Rotterdam, parts of The Hague and other parts of Holland.

Colette and family finally came on board of the ship that would bring them to safety: England. At first the captain would not take Colette's family on board but after pressure from higher officials, he gave in. What a relief this was!

Then there was the trip across the North Sea with German planes flying overhead and continually bombing this vessel fleeing from the Nazis.

What a trip this was! Bombs were raining down all around the ship. The Germans kept this up until the ship passed Hoek of Holland. Miraculously this ship was not hit, notwithstanding the many bombs falling beside it. Apparently the German planes went back to flatten the inner city of Rotterdam. Finally the family arrived in England safe and sound with one little suitcase each. They were happy to be alive and together as a family, but they had lost everything: family, friends, and possessions.

They had to struggle to keep alive the first few days but

Colette's Dad had an income from the government and that continued. They found rooms, at first in boarding houses and then an apartment. The bombing in London became so dangerous that Colette's father looked outside of the city for housing, which was a little better. This meant a longer time to travel to work. In the house they rented was a small grand piano and indeed Colette played it on the weekends.

Colette, who had been a student-teacher in Holland, found office work at the Dutch Government building and at night she studied for her admission diploma for law school.

While working at the Department of Interior Affairs, she met the four lawyers who had been sent from The Netherlands East Indies, (which was named Indonesia after the war with Japan) to help out the Dutch Government in exile in London, England. The Netherlands East Indies, at this time was a colony of the Netherlands and was not occupied by the Germans or by the Japanese yet.

Lawyer number five arrived later and as it happened Dr. Andrew Van Heekeren (the fifth lawyer) was to meet with the Minister at the Department of Interior Affairs. As the Minister had a meeting, he might be a little late to see Andrew Van Heekeren, so he asked Colette to receive him, make his excuses and keep this gentleman waiting for a few minutes.

Dr. Andrew Van Heekeren came at the appointed time and Colette found it very easy to entertain him. Or was she entertained? He was a tall slim man with twinkling brownish eyes and later Colette noticed there were green specks in these brown eyes.

She explained about the lateness of the Minister. Colette had expected Dr. Van Heekeren to be a little older, like the other lawyers. He appeared to be around thirty years old. While waiting Andrew told her some corny jokes and time flew by.

Eventually, several of the Ministers came to meet Andrew and they all went into the main office, where it was decided that Andrew would work at the Department of Finance as he had had already four years of experience in that department in Dutch East Indies.

Colette now had something to think about. She thought, what a happy man! She wondered how he would be in a more difficult situation. Then again I'll probably never see him again as he is going to be working in another building.

Little did she know?

A few days later, to her surprise there was Dr. Van Heekeren standing before her.

"Do you have an appointment with the Minister?" Colette asked.

"No, I thought I'd just visit my friend Richard here and see you of course."

Was she astounded! Of course she brought him to Richard's office, he seemed to expect him. On their way out to lunch they joked a little with Colette and off they went.

From then on Colette saw the three musketeers (Jim, Richard and Andrew) regularly as these three men had become good friends on their long journey from Dutch East Indies to England. They often had lunch together.

Colette started to think rather often about Dr. Van Heekeren, but she did not dare let her thoughts wander about this situation too much. She looked forward to their short lunchtime meetings. These were always full of fun, only a little too short.

One day Richard suggested dinner with Jim and Andrew and then he said "You, Colette, you can bring some girl friends along."

Richard arranged everything. They were to meet at the lobby of the Mount Royal Hotel, which at that time had a rich looking, wide staircase in the lobby.

Many years later Andrew told a friend that when he saw the three girls coming down the stairs, he knew at that moment that he would want to marry Colette and wanted her to be the mother of his children. He described Colette to his friends as not being really beautiful but pleasant to look at, a person who was steady and could be trusted. She had slightly curly blonde hair, large blue eyes and long, long legs. She had a curiosity to see, learn and explore the rest of the world.

They all had a good time that night dancing, eating and talking. The girls wanted to know all about life in Indonesia. The three men described their life in Indonesia: the good, the bad and not to forget the funny.

Richard was not so enamored with life there, but Jim and Andrew had lived most of their lives on Java except for the time they studied at the University of Leiden, so to them it was home.

After this hilarious evening things went back to normal. Dr. Van Heekeren, who had become Andrew since their evening out, still visited Richard now and then and always had a joke ready. Colette tried to ignore her thoughts and feelings about Andrew. She even tried to ignore him now and then or be out of the office when she knew he was coming.

Richard tried to find out how she felt about Andrew, but she showed indifference. After many weeks Andrew asked her out for lunch. He took her to a small but beautiful restaurant, the Mirabelle. The tables had white damask tablecloths and were beautifully set with flowers on each table. They discussed many different things and seemed to enjoy each other's company.

For quite a while Colette did not see Andrew at all and she heard through the grapevine that he was going out with an older woman, who worked in his department. Several weeks passed without any invitations from Andrew. Colette had a little talk with herself: "Just forget about him, if he is interested in others, let him." As if that was easy to do!!

She had to stay home for the next two weeks because the flu hit her very badly. She was not able to continue her studies, as she was exhausted after coming home from the office.

But with spring coming, she started to feel better. Andrew came to see her and asked her out for lunch. This happened more often now. He also asked her out for dinner and dances at night. Colette felt she should say "no."

How could she say this to tall, slim Andrew with his beautiful brownish eyes with green specks and that big smile on his face? He would just look at her and she was lost. They always had such good conversations and they seemed to like the same things as: reading, walking in the fields and forests in Surrey, enjoying nature, playing tennis, and swimming.

They did many of these things together. They began to know each other's thoughts and expectations, their friendship grew. Colette wrote about this in her diary.

Since she was not studying anymore Colette had started to write poetry or as she called them: "musings". She would often write a Haiku at the end of the day.

Although the nuns at her High School had never encouraged her to write, on the contrary her essay marks were generally pretty low, but they had often said: "You seem to have a way with words."

Colette always felt comfortable putting words down and in the office the bosses generally agreed with the correspondence written by her. While teaching later on she always encouraged her students in their writing and occasionally wrote along with her pupils. These little children enjoyed having their teacher write a short story too, or the whole class and Colette together made up a story.

Up to now Colette had done little in this field, as there was not much time to indulge in this past time of writing. Something must have pushed her on though and she wrote several children's stories and musings, about nature and animals. Sometimes she wrote on the way to the office in the train.

Now and then she discussed her writing problems with Andrew. He was very supportive and encouraging; she needed more experience. She had never had much encouragement in this area and now this made her thoughts more whimsical and playful. Her creativity and imagination grew.

During all their conversations it appeared that Andrew was a baptized Catholic, although he seldom attended church. Colette stored that fact away for the time being. She knew that eventually she would want to have a Catholic husband with whom she could bring up their children in their faith.

While Colette's creativity grew slowly and story after story evolved, she began to see where this success came from and that was, encouragement from Andrew and secondly from The Great Creator, inspiring her to write.

In her private thoughts she could see the power of His enormous creation. To get an inkling of this gift of creativity, FAITH is needed, which is the main difficulty for humans, who are so weak and so easily misled in thoughts and deeds.

In the meantime the war with Germany continued. Bombs kept on coming down on London and all over England.

Incendiary bombs were quite a hazard. A voluntary fire brigade was formed. Colette and her father signed up for this. Once a week each one sat on top of the roof of their house with a pump and some buckets of water ready to extinguish eventual fires. This was a lonely scary experience, sitting there in the dark with only a flashlight, which was to be used only in case of emergency. Because of the blackout there were no streetlights, windows were covered up; everything was pitch black to prevent the German pilots from seeing where they could drop their bombs.

Sometimes the Nazis succeeded as when their bombs struck the oil refinery in East London. To Colette it looked like fireworks but it went on for hours.

It seems strange that in those difficult war years one's thoughts, dreams, cravings and purpose of life just went on as normal; that is non-stop. Colette took correspondence courses from the Technical College in journalism, which she found quite interesting.

All the conversations Colette and Andrew had, gave her a good picture of Andrew's way of life and she knew she was falling more and more in love with him. Time would tell and intuition would lead her on.

Andrew told Colette about life in Dutch East Indies, where he was born and what a lovely free life he had had as a child while his mother was still alive. After her death his life became more serious.

He told her about the garden parties and fireworks. In one instance the garden boy (kebon) was to start the fireworks. Everything was explained to the boy, but the fireworks did not light up, and so the boy ran to start it again notwithstanding admonishes to stay back. He was so enthusiastic and enjoyed this lighting party so much, that he went back to it. But the fireworks had a mind of its own and exploded the moment the poor kebon was back. He was in black soot from top to bottom. He was unhurt and even joking but not Andrew, he was pretty worried about the boy Johnny. He appeared later on again making fun of the situation.

Andrew liked Johnny very much and he could see some future in him. One day he made a deal with him. "Johnny," he said, "if you learn to read and write I'll give you a fountain pen."

Andrew found him a teacher. The result was not only a fountain pen, but a job as clerk at Andrew's office.

Colette found Andrew very caring. Little London urchins were never passed by without a gift. Chocolate was rationed, but he tried to have sweets and small money in his pockets at all times.

Of course now and then doubt would set in which would depress her for a while, but she would try to see the situation from Andrew's point of view. He had to be sure, too and for the moment he enjoyed his happy-go-lucky bachelor's life to the fullest.

Life went on. Colette worked in the office during the day and sometimes wrote her poems at night. She was always writing, even though only in her head, when they went for their long walks on the weekends. These weekend outings into the countryside gave her plenty of inspiration. The forests and wildflowers near Guildford were so beautiful.

Colette felt so lucky to be able to discuss her ideas and her writing problems with Andrew, although he saw life more realistically. He had a more scientific mind.

She said to herself: "It is so important to me to be able to discuss ideas, feelings, and beliefs that are sometimes pretty serious and then again occasionally light-hearted, comical and cheerful, but also positive. Andrew could nearly always see the humorous side of the problem or he could turn a difficulty into a joke."

Finally, at least that's what impatient Colette considered, and after a bit of snuggling and smooching, he popped THE question: "What about getting married and living together forever?" Colette who had looked forward to this question for so long did not need any time to answer. She knew with whom she wanted to be with for the rest of her life. Having made up his mind, he was in a big hurry to get married, better tomorrow than the day after!

However Colette's parents could not see why they were in such a hurry. There was this war being fought. Bombs were falling day and night. Many people were killed. Their children might become orphans, as there was a lot of bombing going on all over England. Andrew and Colette had indeed wanted children but to throw them into this insecure world? They discussed this matter quite often. They finally decided not to have children until life seemed more secure and to discuss this again later on.

The parents had their wish, Colette and Andrew would get married in three months time, which seemed like a century to them. At that time coupons were needed for clothes and materials, therefore Colette chose to wear a lovely deep blue dress, made by her mother.

As neither of them had family, other than Colette's parents in England, the wedding became a very small affair with just family and friends which was just as well in wartime.

Andrew sometimes mentioned his unhappiness in his work. He complained, "Those old fuddy-duddies are just managing the office, they could be getting ready for a total change of government in the Dutch East Indies when there will be peace again." From the beginning, he had not liked his work or his bosses. The Dutch East Indies were at that time just starting to talk about freedom and abolishing the colonial ties so he started to look around and put out feelers for a job in another department. Andrew felt that the politicians in London did not understand this movement for freedom. He had friends in Foreign Affairs who were keeping their eyes open for a job opportunity for Andrew.

The offer came after a few months. The Vancouver Dutch Consulate needed someone. Andrew wondered if Colette would want to leave her parents. She did not even think about it. She knew her parents would not like it, but as she said: "I am married to you, therefore they will agree for us to go to Canada together. You are not happy with your work here and I love you, and want to be with you. It is better to move on, but I am glad that we haven't any children to take along on this dangerous journey crossing the Atlantic, where there are so many predatory U boats lying in wait to take an Allied ship down."

After a tearful goodbye and promises of visits to Canada after the war, the young couple left on an empty Canadian troopship to Halifax. Crossing the Atlantic Ocean was more than dangerous. The ship had to zigzag to avoid German U boats that were on the prowl like shark hunting for a fish. The weather was cold and stormy. The ship was tossed up and down and sideways by wind and water.

Then they had to take the long journey by train to Vancouver on the West Coast. This trip went very smoothly. Traveling through beautiful countryside was wonderful. Mountains starkly white with snow beside black rock at some places. At a lower level, dark green trees stood majestically. Neither Andrew nor Colette had ever seen such sights. What a beauty! Coming from war-torn Europe with its destructed, ruined cities and disturbed nights by bombs and air raid warnings, these lovely unspoiled and pristine surroundings, were too much for the writer in Colette. That would come later.

CHAPTER 2

Finally they arrived at the City of Vancouver. Their impression was that this must be the most beautiful city in the world with its flowers, harbors, trees, ships, too much to take in.

The young couple was able to take over the apartment of the former attaché. It was in a rather nice neighborhood with a park close by and there were many different kinds of trees all around. The climate was very wet and chilly, actually not so much different from England.

The next item on the agenda was to get Canadian teaching papers for Colette. She was able to organize one year at Simon Fraser University and eventually she could take summer and evening courses to finish her degree for Bachelor of Education. It was hard to go back to school at first, but Colette enjoyed the relationship with students and profs. They were looking ahead and knew that they would need a good income for their future children's education.

Even though Andrew helped a little in the apartment, there was still plenty of cleaning and cooking to be done, which mostly happened on weekends. Andrew, having grown up in the Dutch East Indies with lots of servants to do the housework, obviously did not know that pajamas could be picked up and folded and not left on the floor. At first this did not appear to be a problem, but after Colette's study as well as cleaning, she got overtired and this lack of cooperation became a serious issue. For a while this young couple went through some serious hardships. These problems were generally resolved by ending up at night in bed, where neither Andrew nor Colette could stay angry.

Sometimes they discussed their differences on their walks along the beach or in the park. Colette said on several occasions: "Why can't you help me a bit? Just pick up your clothes and throw them into the laundry basket or wipe the bath after use. I know I should not yell at you, but when I get tired, I forget." Andrew promised again and again: "I'll try, but I seem to be so tired too. There is this totally new job and I need to put a lot of energy and time into this work." And indeed Colette could see that Andrew did not have as much energy as she had. Andrew wondered: "Maybe we both are having trouble acclimatizing to this new country."

Colette and Andrew had conflicts often enough but as Colette had suffered so much during her childhood from noisy quarrelling parents she had decided early in life to first of all find a quiet, sensitive and most of all a husband who could see the humor in debatable cases. While she grew up she could see the senselessness of all her parents' quarrels. Of course there would come times of thorough disagreements

After Andrew had settled at his job at the Dutch Consulate, he too wanted to get Canadian Law certification. He had his doctorate in law from Holland, but this was in Roman law, while B.C. had Custom Law. He had taken Civil Law, but now he wanted Foreign Affairs as he could see that with so many immigrants and different ethnic groups, foreign affairs could be a good future and International law would be suitable for his job at the Consulate as well.

All this kept them very busy.

The war was still raging on both sides of the world, but there now was more hope for an end to this affair since the Allies had started the near impossible invasion of France (Normandy) and Italy. Too many men lost their lives in this valiant, near hopeless attack by the Allied Troops.

In East Asia, where the Japanese had occupied many countries, the suffering in the Japanese camps continued, as well as the air battles of many islands. Troops, from the U.S.A., Holland, Australia, Britain, Canada and New Zealand were all preparing for the eventual attack in S.E. Asia as soon as the time would be right for this invasion.

In the meantime Andrew and Colette worked hard to achieve their personal goals.

There was not much time or money for relaxation. Even concerts were too expensive except for the occasional free music in the park. They only went to Consulate affairs and walked a lot in the beautiful parks of Vancouver. They had no car, but the walking was enjoyable as well as good for their health. They wandered through Stanley Park and Queen Elisabeth Park and of course they enjoyed the beach.

Colette was lucky to be able to do her student-teaching in the city at least she could be at home with Andrew who was still her number one love.

Andrew had to use his vacation time and weekends for his studies, which he certainly did not like to do. Those two years were rather hard on them, but they had to succeed.

The climate was another story; it was nearly the same as in Holland and England or maybe even wetter. The umbrella was never far away. It was damp, moist and cloudy most of the time, but the temperature did not go to extremes, which was a blessing. When the sun came out the dreary weather was forgotten. There were some lovely sunny summer days, which were used for strolling in the park or seeing different suburbs to find out where they eventually would want to live.

There were the mountains on three sides of the city, with the sea on the west side. In winter, the snowy, white, Mountain View was magnificent. The harbors with their large ocean liners, freighters and ferries were very attractive to Colette, who had always enjoyed seeing those big ships in the Rotterdam harbors. The yacht harbor was a lovely spot although there were not many sailboats around in wartime.

Actually the war was getting worse. The Japanese were expanding their front. The war situation was growing more worrisome. The Japanese seemed to have such an enormous supply of everything: planes, weapons and food. Occasionally a new report came out from the occupied territory where the Japanese had interned all white people. Men were separated from the women and children who didn't get enough to eat. They starved. The Japanese soldiers did not get much more to eat but they were used to very small rations. The men in the camp had to work extremely hard on empty stomachs and they worried about their loved ones. Maybe it was a good thing they did not know that their young daughters and wives were raped and abused or that their children were starving in the camps.

Colette became pregnant. The timing was pretty good as the new baby arrived just a few weeks after Colette obtained her teaching degree. Their little son, Tommy was a sturdy baby, who finally after a few noisy weeks stopped screaming and crying and slowly became a lovely, fairly placid baby. He was very curious, looking around his crib or baby carriage, trying to get his little chubby hands on toys. He looked just like his father. He even had the same square shape of his hands, his light skin and freckles.

His parents were so happy with him. Colette stayed home to watch him grow and develop. They both enjoyed his attention getting antics and his walking or rather running on his sturdy little feet.

Next the climbing period started. He wanted to see everything from the top.

One night Colette woke up hearing noises from Tommy's room. Very softly, so she would not wake up Andrew, as he needed his sleep, she got out of bed and went to Tommy's room. Upon investigation she found him standing on top of his little desk which was under the window. He had put his small chair on top of the desk. He was just starting to climb on the chair when Colette came in and got the shock of her life. Colette caught him in her arms and yelled: "Andrew, come and help."

Andrew hammered the window shut to prevent more accidents.

Tommy tried to help his father with all sorts of building and fixing projects around the apartment. He would be right behind Andrew. Poor Daddy stepped right on his foot, which made him feel so bad that he had hurt his little son. But... Tommy kept on helping.

Little Tommy was quite capable with his small chubby hands. His Dad encouraged him to build at first with wooden blocks and later with the meccano set. Working with screws and bolts was fine motor control. Needless to say he would become the architect he was meant to be.

Andrew had obtained the British Columbia law papers and they decided to stay in B.C. and become Canadian citizens. After five years in Vancouver, he left the consulate and joined the B.C. Department of Justice.

When Tommy was two he got a little sister. Ashley was not such an easy child as Tommy had been. Ashley knew what she wanted right from the beginning and saw to it that she got it otherwise she was fairly reasonable and loveable.

Mama Colette found that playing the piano settled Ashley down. She seemed to listen, relax and fall asleep.

One day a dog followed the family home from the park to their door and decided to stay with the family. She evidently wanted to be adopted. No matter how often she was put outside the door she sneaked in, probably with the help of Tommy, who by then had learned to open doors. He loved that dog and would play with it for hours. This black and white sheepdog was named Kelly.

When Ashley was around two she would sit on her Mom's

lap and tickle the piano keys. Most babies at that age would just hit hard, but Ashley was trying out and listening. She would try to hit harder or softer and listen. At three years old she could pick up a simple tune. Both, Ashley and Colette hummed along with the tune. Both parents could see some talent, which they felt should be explored.

Andrew had played the violin a little in his youth, but after awhile he found he would rather go swimming than study the violin.

One day Andrew came home with a small violin for the five year old Tommy, but like his father he had no real interest or patience. Ashley jumped at it and tried this violin out. She was often discouraged by the sounds it made, and she would go back to her piano.

There used to be outdoor concerts in the park during the summer, which the whole family often attended. Several marches were played here like the "Washington Post" and "Radetzky March" Ashley was totally involved and listening, but Tommy just wanted to run around. They kept him quiet with paper and crayons. That seemed to satisfy him and lo and behold he was trying to sketch trees and people.

After coming home from one of these concerts, Ashley declared one day: "I want to play the violin with an orchestra." She tried hard at home and got so disappointed now and then with the sounds she made. Finally, Andrew suggested a proper music teacher for the violin, while her mother would keep on giving Ashley piano lessons.

The piano is hard to play for tiny fingers. This instrument is actually made for large men's hands. The parents could see the improvement on the piano. Ashley loved to try out her own music. She was only four years old, but she had tenacity and kept on trying to make her own melodies. Andrew suggested a music school, where she could be tutored in both piano and violin. Andrew would have loved to teach her the beginnings of violin, but he had such a busy law practice that he often brought loads of work home. They decided to wait for a little while.

They could see that their bright children would need an education not only academically, but also in arts and music. Colette wanted to stay home with Tommy and Ashley until they were in school. They could foresee large amounts of money would be needed for music lessons and possibly university later on. Tommy was developing a knack for drawing. His grandfather had been a painter, so it was not too hard to see where this came from. A better piano would be needed soon. Their second hand piano had served them well so far but in a few years a grand piano would be needed, and Ashley would outgrow her violin.

In the meantime Colette taught her little daughter piano and a little theory whenever this came up during the short lessons.

The war in Europe had ended a few years ago. Colette had often worried about her parents living in such a dangerous zone. They wrote, but letters were slow to arrive. When peace had been declared they were able to start planning for the parents' visit.

So far everyone was happy and Andrew climbed the ladder at the Department. They had been living frugally and were now able to look around for a house. After a lot of searching, they found a house which looked suitable. They used up all their savings plus they needed a mortgage but they were both so excited about the floor plan as well as a manageable sized, but well laid out garden. This meant a longer commute into the city every morning for Andrew, but the house was exactly what they had wanted with four bedrooms, an office they could share, a large sized living room with a special place for the grand piano that they hoped to buy eventually.

The house was situated a little higher up the mountain, which gave them a fantastic view, especially at night when all the lights were on in the harbor and the Lions' Gate Bridge. What a view!!

It was even better than they had hoped for in their dreams. At that time there was a law that stated that no buildings could be built higher than the present owners' view.

Andrew loved the garden, which was well landscaped and had a rock garden at the end of the yard. Now they had a proper guestroom, so that Colette's parents could be invited to come over from Holland and stay with them. The parents arranged a trip as soon as they could. They came via New York by ship, stayed with friends from the Dutch Consulate in Montreal and then came by train to Vancouver. What a trip this must have been! They kept talking about the beautiful sights they had seen from the train.

What a meeting! Oma and Opa had never seen their grandchildren. They enjoyed, and of course spoilt them as grandparents do. They had had their time and responsibility of parenting, now was the time for enjoying the children.

Tommy loved going for walks with his grandfather, he walked with him down to the harbor, where they looked at the different ships. Opa pointed out the freighters and across the water there were several cruise ships waiting to be loaded with passengers and their luggage, going to Alaska. Upon returning Opa thought it better to take the bus up the mountain. Even from the bus stop there was still quite a climb up to the house.

The new house still needed new curtains and some bedspreads. Oma happened to be a very good seamstress and immediately promised Colette to help her make the new drapes. The two of them went with Ashley to town to buy some bright material. It was a lot of work, but it made an immense difference to the house.

On weekends Andrew would take the whole family up to Whistler Mountain where they saw the tops of the mountains all covered in pure white sparkling snow.

During his holidays in August Andrew rented a trailer and drove the family to Vancouver Island, via the ferry from Tsawassen. The grandparents were so lucky this year. The good weather was holding and was enjoyed by all.

The trip on the ferry to and from the island was the high point of the trip as they all talked about this adventure for a long time afterwards.

Oma treated the children with some Dutch cooking. For instance she made "poffertjes" (pancake balls) or "Oliebollen" which are a kind of doughnut without the hole. They should actually be eaten on New Year's Eve but they tasted just as good in July.

Eventually it was time for Colette's parents to go home. Everyone was sad to see the grandparents leave. After Oma and Opa had departed, the house felt pretty empty. Colette stayed home one more year with Ashley while Tommy attended school.

The teachers there saw quite quickly that Tom was well ahead of his class. Luckily the teacher gave him more advanced work, which he loved. He was so happy and eager about his schoolwork. His teacher had given him a good start and she loved his art work.

The house was rather large; there was plenty of cleaning to do to keep it in order. Colette wanted to do the cleaning herself so they could save enough to pay off the mortgage.

She kept this up until Ashley went to school. Colette found a teaching position in North Vancouver, which luckily was not too far from the house. With her teaching, the housework became a bit too much. She just did not have enough time to clean as Ashley needed to be brought to her music lessons and Tommy wanted to play soccer.

A young Philippine girl named Minah, applied. She seemed to like the children and they in turn liked her. This was a good omen. Minah would come one day a week to clean and offered to take care of the children on the few days that

Colette had meetings and could not be home for the children. Minah soon became part of the family! She would be there at four o'clock to give the children a snack and play with them. She would also start the meal for that evening. A busy lady she was! She was always ready to help Colette out after school hours when needed.

The summer weekends and holidays were mostly spent camping as they now had a small trailer. The whole family enjoyed the great outdoors. At that time the Provincial Parks were very cheap and several of them were free. Parents and children learned a lot about nature from the campfire talks given by the Park officers.

During these camping trips they often met with a couple named Peter and Marion Thompson. As Peter also worked at the Department of Justice, the two men had a lot in common. Peter was a happy go lucky fellow when away from his work, where he seemed to be extremely efficient. He had a photographic memory. This was the reason why everyone at the department knew him. If there were any old cases, Peter would know how to find it.

Peter was forever teasing his wife Marion, who was not shy to repartee. She was a psychologist and had quite a large practice. Peter always joked about her and told his friends that she was always analyzing him. Peter and Marion had no children yet. They were always ready to play with Tommy and Ashley, who adored their adopted Uncle Peter and Aunt Marion. Marion would often say: "Colette, why don't you take a rest while I take the kids for a hike." Tommy and Ashley loved that, because as the children said: "Mom, she knows everything."

That's a lot, but what is everything?" Colette would reply.

"Oh, birds, trees, flowers, even weeds," said Ashley and Tommy added: "and she takes us on secret paths."

During warm weather Andrew took the children swimming, giving Colette a little free time for writing, if the writing-bug hit her.

Being so close to nature the poetry muse liked to appear and Colette had to take advantage of that writing chance. What is more relaxing than the soft, smooth sound of lake water slapping against the shore or waves roaring on to the beach. People who have to live in a large noisy city appreciate this.

When they went out with the trailer Ashley could still play on a small keyboard, where she could do scales or make up her own tunes. Tommy would occasionally play his violin, but his heart was not in it. Tommy was actually a good swimmer for such a little guy. Andrew loved to take him for longer swims to an island. Ashley stayed more with her Mom.

Later when the children became a little older and had homework they did that in the camp also.

After several years Andrew had his greatest wish, they were able to buy a second hand small yacht. As luck would have it they all had sea legs and enjoyed their time on the water. While the children were so young they stayed on the lakes, where the water was calmer than on the boisterous, noisy sea.

Sailing and camping took a lot of their time. They all enjoyed nature, they learned about the birds in the trees, animals in the forest and the flowers. As soon as the children could read there were books about birds, animals and wild flowers in the trailer. The children learned to identify the different species. They enjoyed the antics of the different animals.

Most meals were cooked in the camp, often they ate hamburgers or fish caught in the streams. Andrew cooked these on a small barbecue. He was a very good cook. Ashley started to help her Mom in the kitchen when she was still quite young. She usually made the salad or an easy dessert. Tommy liked to sneak out and often had to be hauled back by Andrew. If he was willing to eat then he should at least set the table.

While camping, it was sometimes difficult to go to Sunday Mass, but they went whenever possible.

Peter and Marion came over one night to tell their friends that Marion was pregnant. They were so excited about that. The two families celebrated this event with a glass of wine.

The damp B.C. climate however, often kept them at home for weekends, during which time house, school as well as garden work had to be brought up to date.

Andrew was on the road to a successful law career. He worked extremely hard as he wanted to succeed for his family, so that the children could have the best education possible.

Tommy had already started to show an interest in drawing, coloring and later painting. As he got older he painted what he saw in nature, if he was sitting down long enough. He was such a lively fellow. Later on his imagination started to work and he would draw castles, buildings and churches.

Andrew's father had been an artist who had painted all his life. He retired early from his business, just to paint for the rest of his life but he never sold a painting. He would say: "Give me a penny and it is yours."

He was seldom satisfied with his work. He often burned his paintings and still after his death there were 400 paintings for each of his six children. Andrew's sister sent these over in several parcels. Some of these decorated Colette and Andrew's house, the rest was stored.

As Andrew said Tommy has that talent from no stranger. They often wondered where this talent would lead. Patience, encouragement and waiting would lead them in the right direction. They encouraged Tommy to try several different hobbies but he mostly grabbed for crayons, pencils or items for building. He always created a new idea for different structures.

Tommy and Ashley had done their First Holy Communion at their parish church in North Vancouver. Catechism was luckily given in their parish on Wednesday night, while the mothers had a CWL meeting and the Knights of Columbus met once a month or they had other meetings that had to do with the church on that night.

This was a very advanced church community where families were kept together and weekends were free for sports, hobbies, camping, or as some needed: sleeping in.

Colette loved teaching. She found that after a long sitting period, a physical exercise break did wonders for the children and their teacher. Surprisingly they quickly settled down knowing there would be another surprise break in the offing.

Colette thought that the students needed to move around more than the teacher. Instead of the teacher walking around and bending over the desks and checking the assignments, the students came to the teacher's desk with their finished work. This encouraged them, because they knew they would be allowed to read or write or do art in their spare time, when the assignment had been finished and corrected.

Every Friday there was a free reading time in the whole school. Colette put on a record of classical, but happy music in the office on the PA system. Teachers, students, and principal, every one, read for half an hour. Amazingly this worked out very well. The students seemed to like it. It looked as if all enjoyed the peace of music and reading during this half hour.

During Phys. Ed. period Colette would sometimes bring her record player and have the pupils march or learn dances. The children liked this.

Music helps students in so many areas. Reading and Math may be improved and team spirit increased when there was music.

Colette found it interesting how differently each child learned. There were some that learned any which way, notwithstanding the teacher. Others had to be prompted and encouraged and often enough they needed to be loved.

Ashley and Tommy did not have problems in school and enjoyed school time, but of course they liked their free time even more and holidays were the best.

Tom, as he wanted to be called now, loved his soccer. As the children grew older and needed more opportunities to socialize and have different activities Andrew enrolled the family into the Sports Club. Mom and Dad could play tennis and meet with other parents, while Tom skated or swam. Ashley did not care very much for volleyball or basketball, she did not want to hurt her hands, but she swam regularly and took tennis lessons.

After sports, Andrew took his family to the cafeteria for a quick bite. Occasionally the children would rather go to McDonald's or for pizza. This eating out was no hardship for Colette as she was not much good in the cooking department. The meals were kept basic, even soup could get burned so easily. Colette usually read a book while stirring and waiting for the ingredients to boil. Then she forgot the cooking. Surprise! Surprise! A burnt offering!

Invention of the microwave was a "God send" and Andrew was a willing helper. Before their marriage Oma had told him he could not expect much enthusiasm or ability in that field. He "thought" he could teach Colette such basics as cooking. Colette tried to encourage their children to cook or bake cookies and left them to it.

Marion was due to have her baby any time. She would be glad to have this over with as her pregnancy had been very difficult. When Peter brought her to the hospital everything appeared to be normal. Whatever happened, Peter never understood. While he was in the room with her the doctor and nurses seemed to be a little worried, then they suddenly became panicky. He was led out of the room and told that everything was OK. He would be called in later again.

Indeed fifteen minutes later, the doctor came to tell him that Marion had died giving birth to a baby-girl and this baby had not survived either. What had happened? Was it a heart attack? That's what the doctor said. Peter was inconsolable. What was he to do for the rest of his life? His whole future his whole life had been arranged around Marion. She was the core of his life. Her death brought such an empty void into his life.

Andrew and Colette were waiting in the lobby for Peter to tell them the news. Colette burst into tears and hugged him when she heard. Andrew paled and put an arm around Peter's shoulder. He did not know what to say. Nothing he could say would alleviate Peter's pain. The Van Heekerens took him to their home until after the funeral. After a few days Peter went home. What was he to do? It all seemed so hopeless. After some time had elapsed Colette offered and then helped him clear the apartment of Marion's clothes and her things. After that he had to try and make a life for himself. He threw himself in his work and the Van Heekerens included him in many of their camping outings and birthday celebrations.

Actually Andrew and Colette missed their best friend too and often mentioned her in their conversations. Now and then they recalled an idea that Marion would have had in a certain case. Even the children sometimes heard the grown-ups talk about Marion and expressed their grief and told Peter how they had always enjoyed camping with Aunt Marion who was such a great science-detective. They said: "Aunt Marion would have taken us out on an expedition and shown us animal paths by following droppings and bird's nests."

Peter's thoughts went back to Marion. What would she say or do in different situations. She had such a clear bright mind. And then he remembered how he always teased her about analyzing him. Then came the idea that she might say: "Pick up your butt and start living, there is no other way out". Now he came along with Colette and Andrew to the concerts he used to attend with Marion as he also enjoyed the music.

Since Peter was so sad and lonely they often asked him over and once a week they had a standing date for supper. He even learned to cook and had the Van Heekeren family over for a meal. Colette would bring the dessert and Andrew always offered a bottle of wine. Peter being from Scottish parents liked to be frugal. He did his own cooking. He certainly looked after the pennies.

As soon as Uncle Peter came into the house for dinner, the children had him involved. "Hey Uncle Peter are you going to play cards with us, or dominoes? Dad said not to bother you, but you like playing, don't you?"

Now and then Uncle Peter brought a surprise game for them. He enjoyed himself as much as the children. The kids were mostly lying down on the floor when playing and Uncle Peter would be right there on the floor with them.

Peter encouraged Andrew: "Come on Andrew here is a space for you; you can join us in this battle."

CHAPTER 3

As Ashley grew so did her musical talents. She took piano lessons from a Conservatorium certified teacher, who not only taught her piano, but also all the different emotions and expressions that can be shown in music. She still played the violin regularly to keep her skills up to par. She really liked this instrument a lot and later on she would see its possibilities.

Starting Junior High, Ashley became very much involved in all the musical activities offered such as choir, doing musicals and then band. With her feel for music she wanted to know all about playing different instruments. Her curiosity made her want to learn more about the wind instruments. She took band classes. This opened up a whole new world for her. Up to now her lessons had been mostly for classical music, the young students demanded modern music with more beat to it. Drums and percussion instruments took care of that. Ashley thought: "You never know whether or not I can use this knowledge, either for playing or for composing." Unknowingly she had her hand on nearly everything connected with the orchestra. She found that she also loved the Saxophone. Later on when she became really good at that instrument she entertained her fellow students by playing solo.

By that time Tom and Ashley were old enough to go occasionally to the Vancouver Symphony with their parents. All enjoyed this family outing and often Peter came along too.

He did not play an instrument, but he loved hearing good music.

Time passed too fast and soon it was time to think of higher education. Tom knew quite early on that he was artistic, but also fairly technical. He wondered what he should take Engineering or Architecture. He decided on Architecture, where he could use his art and build at the same time.

He applied for scholarships and obtained one for the University of B.C. The parents were happy with this choice, as they wanted to keep him at home a little longer if possible. They loved him so much. Boarding and traveling expenses could be saved by living at home. This architecture course was going to be very expensive and although Andrew and Colette had good jobs, Tom would have to help out with part-time jobs. He was willing enough, but now the summer vacations would be without Tom, this, the parents disliked, but their children were growing up!! Friends started to interfere and Tom would rather stay in Vancouver on the weekends to be with them.

Even Ashley wanted to stay home and go out with "boyfriends". Andrew found this an impossible and a distasteful word. How could his darling daughter want to go away from him?

Mama Colette, though she did not like that part of the growing up, could see that Ashley and Tom needed to socialize. The school as well as the Sports' Club gave them plenty of opportunities. So the worrying time had come for the parents. Could they stay away from alcohol?

Andrew and Colette had openly discussed this problem with their children as to what might happen at parties. Now they had to leave it to the youngsters to handle these situations. All through their young lives the parents had mentioned "character". "You are your own person, you do not follow others." Alcohol was discussed and they were told to phone home anytime if there were difficulties.

On Tom's graduation night, Tom was allowed to use his

Mom's little car. This car was hit in the parking lot of the hotel where the festivities were held.

When some years later Ashley graduated from High School the parents brought their daughter and two girlfriends to the hotel, where the graduation celebration was held and picked them up when they phoned to say that they were ready to come home. Some of the graduates had been drinking liquor, which was the reason the girls phoned and they got out before anything happened.

Now there were two children at UBC, which was quite an expense even with the help of scholarships. Now the time had come when the youngsters were no longer interested in camping and going out with their parents. They had their own friends and activities.

Andrew thought it wiser to sell the trailer, but they kept their small sailboat. The two of them could enjoy this, themselves.

At home, tall blond Ashley talked about her music professor, only mentioning what a wonderful violin teacher he was and could he play!! He was also concertmaster in the Vancouver Symphony. He was going to organize a small orchestra at the U. where Ashley played mostly piano, but she had kept up with her violin studies as well. She had a very busy schedule.

One day Colette overheard Ashley and her friends discussing the new prof. Not only was he just a good violinist, who could make the highest notes sing on his violin, but as the girls were exclaiming: "He's just gorgeous, with curly black hair, straight nose and so tall! He must be more than 6'2".

After the girls had left Colette tried to bring up the subject of this good-looking prof, but all Ashley said was: "Yes, he is good looking, but ever so arrogant!"

The subject was now closed. Ashley never talked about him, but when asked how her violin classes were going; the answers were short and to the point. "Fine and interesting." or "oh, he is a good teacher and his playing is out of this world. I am learning so much from him."

Ashley had boy-friends and girl friends that came to the house but she never talked about or brought home a special friend. As a mother Colette was of course curious, but she never learned more about her daughter's relationships.

Ashley was now in her last year at UBC; she had just finished her practice teaching and was ready to graduate. She had already applied and obtained a job as a Junior High music teacher in a Burnaby school for the following year.

The graduation and party were a great success.

Although Ashley never talked about her good looking prof, she apparently knew him better than she let on. At the reception after the graduation and award ceremony she introduced Dr. Mark Maxwell, her music prof, to her parents. Colette immediately felt there was something in the air. She mentioned this to Andrew later on, but of course he had not noticed anything.

Later on though, they saw Ashley and her prof. on the dance floor several times.

Colette repeated: "Something is going on."

Ashley, however, remained silent about him.

After a restful holiday everyone went to work or study in September. Tom had been working all summer for the same architectural firm as last year. Encouraged by his employers he was now going for his Master's degree in Architecture.

Ashley started her job as a Junior High teacher, half time teaching English and half time music. On Saturdays she took violin and piano lessons towards her Masters degree in Music.

Was Ashley meeting Mark Maxwell there? She didn't mention him at all. The parents knew she took violin lessons from him, but did she see him socially? Colette had an inkling of an idea that her daughter saw her prof. more than she let on. Colette thought she probably was not very sure about him.

Ashley was working many hours with the Junior High band. The students enjoyed their practices, which was exactly Ashley's idea: to bring over the joy, hope, love and freedom that music may express. It may express beauty as portrayed in the "Cavalleria Rusticana."

At the end of that first year of teaching the band gave a performance for the students' parents. The result was rather good for their level. Having had one year of practice, this promised a good future for the following year.

Ashley had taught herself a way of accompanying the band while playing the piano and conducting at the same time.

Although Ashley was pretty happy teaching Junior High, she found after a couple of years that she would rather teach music and band at the High School level. In this way she would be able to see and use the results of her teaching in the lower grades. She could then go into music for more mature students and she would be able to go to competitions with them.

Indeed she obtained a position as musical director at the High School. She followed a director who was known for his work on musicals and operettas. This was going to be a real challenge, which she loved and needed. She was still growing in this field. She saw so many opportunities and outlets for her talent.

This first year of teaching High School music took an enormous amount of preparation and she wanted to keep up her own piano and violin lessons. She had a great amount of energy, which certainly helped her. But that first year was very hard, even though her mother tried to help as much as possible. Colette, who was teaching slow learners and music in the middle school, understood the difficulties and frustration in Ashley's work.

The second year of teaching at the High School went so much better. Ashley knew the students now and their background. She even started to bring a little bit of classical music in, but only the kind of music which could bring joy, to the teenagers. Mostly she introduced lively marches, dances and lighthearted melodies. She also worked on some rap and rock which most of the youngsters enjoyed.

Even with all her preparation for her classes, sometimes after school hours and lunchtime rehearsals, Ashley continued her violin and piano lessons on Saturdays. Her violin prof was still the same tall, slim, curly black-haired with hazel eyes, Dr. Mark Maxwell.

Clearly Ashley saw more of her prof then she let on at home. Only much later did Colette and Andrew hear about the lunch dates after classes on Saturdays.

When Colette suggested that Ashley bring this man home for Sunday dinner, she did not answer. Ashley was not too sure about this relationship.

She told her Mom that she liked him very much and that they had so much in common in the music field. During their lunches together, they had such good conversations about the different instruments, the various kinds of music and they found they had the same appreciation of nature and the expression of music and emotions. They discussed how natural beauty affects the reaction of all art. Writing as well as painting, composing and playing instruments is often inspired by fascinating or peaceful land or seascapes, flowering fields and blooming orchards.

Music is for many people like a heavenly painting; it touches deep emotions.

She told her mother all this but he was still her prof. and Ashley told her that she found this a difficult and confusing relationship.

Then there was the fact that there were numerous young women attending Dr. Mark's classes. She heard them talking about his good looks and easy going manner, etc. which made it harder for Ashley's confidence. Was she one of many? Was she just a pleasant and interesting part time date?

Their friendship was growing. Mark now told her more

about his background. He was from Irish descent and R.C., although since Mark was living on his own in an apartment on the North Shore overlooking the harbors and shipping, he did not attend church very often, only with his family on holidays or particular occasions such as the baptisms of his nieces.

They discussed technical, musical knowledge and how to combine this with sound and feelings.

Ashley mentioned her love for directing the school band. Dr. Maxwell told her that, he was the concertmaster at the Vancouver Symphony and: "I would love to conduct an orchestra playing light classical music, which many more people will enjoy, for instance the "March of the Toreadors" or Strauss's "Empire Waltz" and some light romantic music by Chopin as "Barcarolle."

That summer Dr. Mark Maxwell taught at the Sorbonne in Paris, while Ashley took more violin, piano and music theory classes towards her Masters' degree. She was very busy, but she felt lonely. She discovered that Mark was often on her mind. She missed their conversations and his jokes. He seemed such a happy man with an even temperament.

Ashley thought his contentment and cheeriness shows in his music and his way of teaching. I am actually learning much more than violin playing.

It did not help that Ashley's parents were traveling in Europe, making it very quiet at home, even though Tom, Ashley's brother was there. He was working that summer again for the same architectural firm he had worked for before, in order to make enough money to help pay for his Master's degree in Architecture.

He was lucky to have this job, even if it was starting at the bottom of the ladder, but he could learn the basics from experienced men and learn the reality of working in this field. His employers were quite happy with his previous work and noticed his potential. They saw a promising future for him and their firm.

Tom was lucky to be able to live at home otherwise he would have had to pay for room and board, which would have made it near impossible to continue his studies. His parents were more than willing to help out, but Tom tried to be independent.

CHAPTER 4

Peter Thompson, who had never found another lady to love, still lived alone in his nice apartment. After a few years since his wife's and baby's death, Peter thought he should give part of his life to the Church and become a Deacon. He still worked at the same office as Andrew. He had been doing very well in his job at the Department of Justice. He had made several promotions, just as Andrew did and he knew that he was always welcome in the Van Heekeren house. In the olden days in Europe Andrew as well as Peter would have been a Right Honorable, but nowadays things were more relaxed and those titles were not used any more. His salary as well as Andrew's had increased accordingly.

Colette was earning a decent salary as a teacher. She had sent several of her children's stories to different publishers but so far the answers were unfavorable. She was often disappointed but she would not give up. She kept sending her stories to other publishers until she heard of an agent who was actively looking for new authors. The agent had found an artist, Caroline Bromley, who really knew how to bring out the essence of the story with her pictures and this made children want to read. She became Colette's friend and collaborator.

Andrew and Colette were now able to satisfy their love of antiques. They enjoyed going to auctions and looking at the antique furniture. In Europe too, they loved going to museums and castles. In Vancouver, occasionally they attended estate sales and tried to bid if they thought they could afford that particular piece of furniture and if it would fit in with what they had.

On one of their visits they had been able to buy a table with six Chippendale chairs, which suited their large sized dining room. They hoped to find two more matching chairs on a later expedition. Earlier they had bought a small inlaid table from Florence.

When they had bought the house so many years ago they had furnished it very simply and sparsely, as they always hoped to furnish the villa as it should be furnished. As they said: "One thing at a time and no debts except for the house mortgage."

With all their ambitions, family and work commitments there was not much time for entertainment. Just occasionally they would go out for supper to a friend's place or have some friends at home, but the effort of making a big dinner was often too much. Lately the two children helped a little which was an advantage. Even now that the children were adults Andrew and Colette felt that they should be at home just in case they needed advice or a shoulder to lean on. Dinnertime was such a good occasion for discussions. They always seemed to have good conversations, even though Tom never lost his annoying teasing streak. And most often Ashley was his target. She often burst out in tears.

Colette and Andrew actually loved to stay at home and enjoyed each other's company. Their love had not diminished during the years of bringing up their children and working hard, on a certain level it had increased. During and after dinner they sat companionably together. Colette was either writing another story or doing schoolwork.

Andrew always had lots of briefs to go over. They would discuss their problems and sometimes argue about their children or with them.

Andrew's friends often remarked that they stayed home

too much. But as Colette said: "We really enjoy our off-spring so much that we don't feel staying at home is a sacrifice and we are so lucky as to love being at home together, relaxing or working on our hobbies. We have so many interests that we are never bored."

It was now Ashley's last year of study for her Master's degree. In the meantime her students in school kept her attention full throttle. There were several performances to prepare. First came Christmas, then the school band had to show off their progress at Easter and finally at the end of the year came the performance of the musical.

Early in the year Ashley had discussed with her colleagues which show would be best and most likely to be enjoyed by the students. It had to be a show that had not been done before in this school and would give enrichment to most students and it had to correlate with several subjects as geography, drama, art, culture etc.

The choice fell finally on Roger and Hammerstein's *The King and I.* The staff had several meetings dividing the different parts to study. *The King and I* was a musical masterpiece. It would give students and teachers a wonderful outlet for art in the form of costumes and stage design.

The Industrial arts department could do stage construction and carpentry. A choir was formed and soloists had to be chosen for the different tunes as: "Getting to Know You," "I Whistle a Happy Tune," and "Hello, Young Lovers" with the choir as background.

The gym teacher was immediately ready to teach the dances, especially for the song: "Shall We Dance."

There were so many opportunities for learning in this musical, even psychology came to the forefront when it was pointed out so cleverly in this play that not everyone can have his own way in life and that stubbornness is only good to a degree.

The teachers were such a compatible group that year. They

worked together and suggested several improvements as they saw it. Of course so much depended on the principal who was caring and cooperative and of course there was a kink somewhere. But there are always disappointments when so many people work together. This one teacher felt sick too often when there were extra duties to be performed. But somehow they all took it in their stride.

The geography teacher taught about habits and clothing as well as culture and social habits in that area of Siam. Life at the Royal court too was studied, as well as the changes the modern world brought to that area.

The English teacher of course taught the Drama part and worked together with the Art and Home Ec. Departments. The young enthusiastic students worked so well with the instructors. Laughter was heard not only in the Staffroom but in classes and hallways.

In between teaching academics and organizing for the special occasions during the year the whole high school worked in parts for the preparation of *The King and I.*

Ashley was kept pretty busy with this project and she loved this work. Happy eager people to work with helped so much. She often thought what a good thing it was that they had started discussing and working on this project so early in the year.

Her own studies kept her on the go and as Colette found out, the Saturday lunches had started soon after Dr Mark had returned again from his stint in Paris. The first Saturday after his return from teaching at the Sorbonne, Dr. Mark asked Ashley "Did you miss me?"

This question came rather as a shock to Ashley. She thought am I to give myself away after three months of his absence? She did not want any sympathy or pity. But she said: "A little, but I was so busy preparing for the new school year and working on my dissertation I had no time to think of anything else."

"Miss Ashley I'll be honest with you, I missed you a lot. I missed our conversations, your laughter, jokes and the ideas you have in teaching and music. Could we see more of each other and see where this friendship leads to?"

Ashley agreed and said: "Yes, we could meet more often and get to know more about each other."

The question now was how? During the week both were so busy. Ashley knew that her mother always cooked a large roast on Sundays or sometimes she ordered in food. Dr. Mark could come in the afternoon and then stay for dinner.

"Yes, let's see how we go from there, and will you call me Mark when we are away from the college?" Ashley agreed to this.

Andrew and Colette were surprised by the announcement that Dr. Mark Maxwell was coming for dinner the next Sunday. They agreed: "Sure, let's have him over for dinner."

Tom would immediately have started to tease his sister as he used to, but Papa Andrew took him to task before hand: "For once stop the teasing, you know how shy Ashley is and you could embarrass her with your jokes and clowning around. Let's get to know Ashley's friend first."

Ashley used to flee to her room crying after Tom's incessant teasing. This was the time that Colette and Andrew had their biggest quarrels. Colette was often on the defense for her daughter which Andrew thought was silly and would defend Tom which was an opportunity for Andrew and Colette to have a fight. Ashley being such a shy sensitive creature found these circumstances upsetting and promised herself that she would try to avoid these situations.

Indeed Tom behaved perfectly the first few times. After the introductions the conversation moved along easily, oiled along with a nice glass of wine.

Colette asked Andrew one day: "Doesn't Ashley look pretty and happy? She looks better than ever, if that is possible."

Andrew agreed. As parents they hoped that Ashley would find a suitable mate and be as happy as they were.

Mark came over several Sundays in a row and everything seemed okay with the two young people. There was a pleasant atmosphere at dinnertime. Mark joined in easily with Tom and Andrew's jokes.

Then for the next two or three weeks there was no Mark. Ashley did not say much at home, just: "He can't make it. There seems to be some family gathering going on at his parents' house."

Ashley had not been invited. Another two Sundays went by and still there was no Mark. Ashley did not look so happy anymore. Finally Colette plainly asked and Ashley sadly said: "I don't know Mom, when he left that last Sunday, we seemed happy and he kissed me and I have not seen or heard from him since. I had a fast glance of him Saturday at the U. I am afraid that's all it was, just a casual friendship. He has lots of girls and women friends to choose from. One of my friends told me he'd been seen going out with a young Math Prof. But why did he tell me that he had missed me so much during his time in Paris?"

This was the big question? Evidently he was not as trustworthy and dependable as he seemed to be.

With the Christmas concert coming up and her thesis to write, Ashley was kept very busy. She tried to forget him, which was not easy. A picture of his face often appeared in her mind.

Tom helped her along by asking her to join him and his friends for Saturday lunch after classes, which she used to have quite often with Mark. Now she joined Tom and his friends. Sometimes one of the profs, from the Architecture department came along. After a few weeks Tom's prof. Dr. Whittaker joined them on a regular basis. After a few of these meetings, he started to single Ashley out but as Ashley said to her brother: "I am not at all interested in him."

From then on she went straight home after her Saturday morning classes and so there was no chance to meet either Mark or Dr. Whittaker.

It was a good thing that Ashley was so busy with her own studies and her school preparations. The musical *The King and I* was coming along nicely. Parts and solos were given out. Choruses and the different instrumental groups were organized. With this busy life she was often able to push all thoughts of Mark on the back burner. She actually was so disappointed in him; she knew that she really cared for him. She had thought that these feelings came from both sides.

However nothing could be done about it. She was already thankful that during this last year of her studies Mark was not teaching her. She could avoid him now. Although he was on her committee for directing and passing her dissertation she was not worried. She knew that he was a fair man and would eventually not let his feelings stand in the way of an objective decision, whatever his feelings for Ashley would be.

What were his feelings? She never saw him now and he didn't come to look for her either. Ashley still felt very hurt. Maybe she had thought too much of him and his emotions did not correlate with her ideas.

They had so often discussed their future in music, but it seemed Ashley had been wrong. She was disappointed not only in Mark but also in herself. Had she misread his attitude and feelings for her? True he had spoken of friendship, but the kisses and conversations had led her to think of a closer relationship. Had she been too eager? She needed to begin a new life. She would first concentrate on the musical and her dissertation for her master's degree.

There was a lot of research to be done, but the project was coming along well. She did not mind the hard work at the moment. She was strong and had her mind set on proving how different composers, conductors and musicians made their music, the way instruments speak to their listeners and how this music brought out emotions such as sadness, melancholy, happiness, and cheerfulness.

Most of all Ashley tried to show how different kinds of music might bring joy, excitement, and happiness to people, just as she tried to teach in her classes. The students came to her classes with more eagerness as they progressed.

Part of her dissertation was about how to teach music appreciation as she had so often discussed with Mark. So many of the young people only liked either Rock, Metallic or Country and Western music, which is okay, to start off with, but Ashley wanted them to learn and appreciate different kinds of music, to feel the joy or sadness expressed in music, like "Wind Beneath My Wings".

As the famous composer Franz Lehar said: "I want to go directly into the heart of the people".

Teaching her classes Ashley would say: "You can see this clearly when you look at the faces of the people during a concert or during a musical show, they seem drawn together. You can see lovers look at each other, showing their love with their eyes as well as their enjoyment and appreciation of the music. Listening to lively waltzes or polkas, don't you feel you want to reach out to each other and dance away? Your feet are waltzing already."

Ashley had many CD's to give examples to the young people. Sometimes they listened or played the different examples of how rhythm, tempo, loud or soft, slow or fast could bring a different atmosphere and another impression of the music they were hearing or performing. She explained how music could show depth and sensation. Fast, exaggerated speed could give hilarious cheerful, high spirits.

She showed them how nature makes music in its own way.

"Listen to the noisy, deafening sound of the waterfall, as it cascades down the mountains; the total silence during a thick fog or the intense noise during a thunder storm or the ocean's thundering waves. Birds make music, some better than others! Bees' zooming is sometimes copied by choirs humming.

She demonstrated to them how the different instruments give character to music. She might play the violin to let them hear the romance and warmth, the harmony and beauty which only a gifted violinist can get out of this instrument.

What a deep feeling is in this instrument as for instance in the song: "I Will Follow Him" and then the contrast that follows.

The violin is like a password to many different worlds.

Of course the students loved the heartbeat of the percussion instruments. At first the teens would bang loud and any which way until Ashley would show them the different sounds and the feeling that can be brought out with these musical instruments.

There is an instrument for every expression. Some of the students loved the wind instruments giving power, spirit and energy. They are so suitable for marches. Ashley had that year two youngsters who played the piano and she knew how to make good use of their playing as well as encouraging them to study in this field. They experienced that with more study came the desired improvement.

Since Mark was now out of the picture, Ashley had only her parents with whom to discuss plans and problems. Her mother Colette, being a half time music teacher at the elementary level understood her difficulties of bringing appreciation of music over to youngsters who are brought up so often with loud, ear-piercing sounds from TV and radio.

Ashley as well as her mother wanted the students to learn and enjoy different kinds of music. And indeed they were rather successful in converting many at first into listening and some even became so devoted that they volunteered to join the band.

Occasionally, mother and daughter found pupils with a musical background. They encouraged these students by letting them accompany the choir and band. Ashley would put the accompanying setting into an easier level, so that beginners would be able to play and at the same time this would encourage the student to play and study. Very seldom they found a violinist among the students. If that happened, Ashley would bring in her violin and play along with the student, thus encouraging him or her to keep on studying.

Ashley saw to it that in the performance of *The King and I*, there was an opportunity to play for soloists or small groups, accompanying the choir and band.

But working with the different instruments, groups in the choir or soloists took an enormous amount of time. For this lunch periods, and after school time was needed, for teachers as well as students. Students at first balked at having to give up free time, but farther on in the year they could see the results of their hard work. There was a lot less of that complaining, if it was there at all.

In preparation for Easter celebration, just before the Easter vacation started, Ashley had found a suitable score for Handel's *Hallelujah.* The trumpets would shine in that beautifully, which the students really enjoyed and the choir was working out well in this performance.

This Easter break was a good opportunity for Ashley to put the last touches on her thesis, which both Andrew and Colette had edited for her.

She never saw or heard from Mark. She often wondered out loud: "What is happening to him?" "Should she phone him and ask whether she had done something wrong? But then he apparently does not want to be in contact with me."

She did not want to embarrass herself. Obviously the friendship was not as strong as Ashley had imagined. She decided to keep things the way they were and hope for the best. She was convinced something had happened!!

She missed the conversations they had and the jokes they shared. Mark was such an upbeat guy. He could see the good in most people. She missed his opinions about all kinds of different musical expressions, concerts, and composers. There were so many things in which they shared mutual interests.

Besides these communications there were, she thought, deeper feelings for each other and now so suddenly there was nothing. No Mark!

She told herself that she would try to forget him. This was easier to plan, but not so easy to do. And now the convocation stood before her door. Would Mark be there? He had to be there as he was in the committee for judging the thesis.

Ashley's parents were so proud of her and had taken time off to be at the convocation. She could not disappoint her parents and skip this event.

Ashley had worried needlessly, everything went smoothly. Mark indeed was in the line of different profs who had taught these graduating students. All the profs were there to hand them their certificates and congratulate them.

Mark shook her hand and wished her well, just as he did with the other students. But what did it cost Ashley to go through this action? She was suffering at the sight of Mark, but did she show any weakness? She came up the stage with a steady pace and put on her usual friendly smile, but she did not make eye-contact. She would not show any feelings!

Colette and Andrew saw the proceedings with sadness in their hearts for their wonderful daughter. They were so proud of the way Ashley carried this situation off with style and courage.

Andrew took his family and Peter, who had also taken time off for this celebration, out for a lovely dinner at the Country Club to celebrate the occasion. Tom came in a little later carrying a fairly large parcel. After dinner Andrew, Colette, Peter and Tom gave her the present. Was she surprised!!

When Ashley saw the present she cried out: "Oh Mom and Dad how can I ever thank you!"

She immediately saw the quality of this beautiful violin.

She kissed both her parents. Even Tom suffered his thank-you kiss, which he took in with his usual jokes. It was one of the better violins on the market. Andrew was joking that maybe it would be a Stradivarius for her doctoral degree. Ashley knew that this particular violin had put her parents back for a couple of thousand dollars. She saw in this present not only the love her parents had for her, but also the encouragement.

They knew she would continue to grow in the musical world.

The next day at school she was surprised to see a lovely bouquet on her desk with a card from the staff and band members. She had brought her parents' present to school to show her colleagues but when she saw the flowers from the students she knew that they were interested in her career as well. She brought out her new instrument and of course had to give a demonstration and show the craftsmanship and the beautiful mellow and romantic, emotional sound this instrument could make.

Now the only big event for Ashley was the performance of the *King and I.*

Each department in the high school had worked on this musical during the year and since Easter all the parts and pieces had come together and that was a big job. Everyone enjoyed the challenge of working together. There was cooperation from the administration to the caretakers, students and parents and the whole staff whether or not they were involved in teaching the different parts or in the makeup department or the stage design etc. This does not always happen in every school. There usually were several complainers, but they certainly were lucky this year.

For Ashley, these last few weeks in May and June were nearly full time *The King.* After school hours, lunchtime rehearsals with the different groups of students, meetings with the staff re: academic subjects and final exams. The end of the school year is usually quite hectic so they tried to keep everything as normal as possible.

There was this musical, but the academic schoolwork had to come first. Scholarship awards and prizes needed to be organized, which again meant meetings with charitable organizations as Rotary, Women's Institute, Hospital Volunteers and businesses had to be contacted for donations. Lists of average marks had to be produced and student's leadership and sportsmanship qualities had to be judged.

Debating clubs had to be adjudicated. This year they kept the music competitions with other schools to a minimum, because everyone was putting all their energy in *The King.* Finally the musical was performed. Parents, teachers, school board members were all amazed at the outcome. It was very nearly professional. The audience gave the performers a standing ovation.

The biggest surprise was that the academic work of the school as a whole had come out with higher marks and better accomplishments were achieved than ever before. The staff felt the students to be really alive and active, not, as so often used to be the case "bored" with everything. There was a certain upbeat atmosphere at the school.

The School board's President remarked on this fact. He said: "It shows that with extra-curricular activities, the academic subjects have been improving, and more students are planning to continue their education. Very interesting! I need to think about this"

This remark plus her own ideas on music and music therapy started Ashley off on a new train of thought. She began to think of doing some research in that field. She planned to look into this after the holidays.

The summer holidays had arrived and as Ashley had saved up enough money, she took a well deserved extended vacation. She traveled to France and stayed two weeks in and around

Paris. She visited the Eiffel Tower, and as many museums, palaces and art galleries as she could. Then she drove north and looked around in Belgium from where her Dad's parents originated.

Then she went on to Brabant in the Netherlands, where Colette's mother's forefathers had lived during the 1500's. Later they had moved to Delft to become the artists in the Delft blue pottery factory.

In Amsterdam Ashley followed an intensive four-week course in orchestra directing. She enjoyed this course and she knew that she would be able to use this knowledge in her teaching in the coming semester. As a matter of fact she got such a pleasure out of this course that she wanted to see what she could do with it. Her prof in Amsterdam told her that she had a real aptitude for conducting as she picked up the different sounds of the instruments so well and knew how to position the musicians in respect to the acoustics in the hall. This course also gave her new ideas for the future. But that was for later when she had all the qualifications and experience she needed. Indeed directing an orchestra and/or choir looked very interesting.

CHAPTER 5

Mark Maxwell, Professor of Music at the University of British Columbia and first violinist at the Vancouver Symphony at 35 years of age, had done very well for himself. His career seemed well established as Professor and concert master. He enjoyed his job at the university immensely. He had a good rapport with the young students. Most girls liked this good-looking prof. He knew how to bring humor to his classes as well as enjoyment for different kinds of music.

He was tall and slim, had black curly hair and soft hazel eyes, which the ladies in his classes certainly appreciated. But he treated male and female with the same and equal good humor. He never singled out any of his students until Ashley was in her last year of her Master's study, then he joined her group in the cafeteria for lunch on Saturdays and from then on he made it a regular date. He made it a point to sit beside Ashley but everyone at their table joined in the conversation. This weekly meeting continued until the summer holidays when Mark went to Paris to teach at the Sorbonne, and Ashley took another subject towards her Master's degree.

Mark's family was very academically oriented. They were rather surprised with their son's choice in the music field, although they should have seen how he had always chosen the violin above sports, academics or other art subjects.

His father was a Justice at the Provincial court; his pretty mother was a Pediatrician with a large practice. One brother, James had followed his father's footsteps and was connected to a well-known law firm; he had recently gotten married. The eldest sibling Sean was now forty years old and taught law at Simon Fraser University. He also was married and had two small children. Sean's wife stayed at home to give the children the best start possible and all the attention they would need.

Everything was going well for the Maxwell family. Each member was working hard and successfully until James got embroiled into a legal scandal.

A rich client had died and the inheritor, who did not agree with the way the will had been set up, accused James of defrauding and bilking the account. The accuser immediately made it into a huge scandal and brought in the paparazzi, which the whole Maxwell family found hard to take. The newspapers made a big deal of this case: a well known lawyer, son of a judge and medical doctor had defrauded this poor man. He needed a good lesson. Exposure was the first thing that would teach him a lesson.

The happiness in this family vanished. The usual laughter and bantering was mostly hidden by worries for one of their own.

Of course, only the best defense lawyer and private investigator were brought into this case, but they all knew that it would take a long time for this case to be solved and the papers loved scandals like this. Some tabloids seemed to enjoy hurting whole families.

Mark was so, supportive of his brother, just as the whole family was, but he did not know what to do. Here he was going out with that lovely girl, whose father also was connected with the law, although in a different area.

What would this scandal do to their relationship? He did not want any trouble for them too.

Mark loved his brother and was convinced of his innocence. He did not know how to go about his relationship with

Ashley. For several Saturdays he had managed to stay away from their usual meeting place at the cafeteria. This he found hard to do. He discussed this relationship with his parents and they agreed that it might be better not to see so much of Ashley, but maybe discuss the reason for not seeing her in order to protect her and her family. Justice Maxwell wondered whether the girl had tried to get in touch with Mark. She had not. Mark thought she knows where my office is. Not for a moment did any Maxwell member think that Ashley might not know of their troubles.

The Van Heekeren family had advised their daughter to stay away from Mark, because if he had really meant it when he mentioned friendship then the contact should be coming from his side. She should keep her head up. At that point Andrew knew nothing about the fraud case. All they saw was how unhappy and disappointed Ashley was.

However after a few days Andrew understood the whole case better. He had seen Mark's last name in the papers. He talked about this to Colette and they wondered if the "culprit" could possibly be a member of Mark's family.

Wasn't it strange that Ashley never mentioned Mark or his family? Did she know about the crime that supposedly had been committed?

The parents noticed that there was not the same spring in her step; she was a lot quieter than usual.

After a month or so Colette being curious and concerned asked her daughter straight out: "Ashley, what is happening with Mark? You don't talk about him. Didn't you see him regularly on Saturdays?"

"Mom, I don't know what is going on. He is never around anymore. He seems to avoid me. He said he wanted friendship and you saw him those few Sundays at home. I think you and Dad liked him too. He seems to be of a good family, although he never spoke much about them. I could go and see him in his office, but do I want to be snubbed?"

Colette agreed that if he wanted to see her, Mark knew where to find Ashley.

Then Andrew came home one night and broke the disturbing news to Colette. As soon as they had a chance to be alone he started off by saying: "Do you remember that long weekend when our family went camping and had that fantastic trip to the Sechelt peninsula with that little side trip admiring the Skookunchuck Rapids? Everything had fallen in place that weekend. Tom and Ashley made a big effort to go on this camping outing with us. The weather was just right. We were three days without worry, without work problems and it probably would be the last long weekend before the weather would cool down and none of us would have time for such an outing again. We just brought the little radio, but we apparently did not listen to the news. I believe Ashley still does not know about the troubles of the Maxwell family and I don't know if we should tell her or not. She is sad but she seems to be taking it in her stride. While we were away TV and papers made a big to do about a lawyer James Maxwell who had allegedly defrauded and swindled a legacy from a business man. The papers immediately took sides with the business man. The man, being the only nephew of the deceased, had expected the whole inheritance."

All the uncle's money and possessions were according to the will, to be given away to charities upon his death. James Maxwell, his lawyer, had assisted the uncle making up the will and followed the uncle's instructions. The whole estate and properties were to be invested and the interest used for scholarships for University students who had entered their medical studies. The student had to sign that he or she would practice for five years not just in Canada but in a rural area in the province of British Columbia.

All this caused a scandal. James and of course the whole Maxwell family suffered under this accusation. Father Maxwell, being a justice, understood the problems of this claim only too well.

That the nephew was upset at losing so much money was possible, but to immediately go to court and accuse the uncle's lawyer of defrauding and on top of it bringing in all the newspapers and TV people, that was a bit strange and overdoing it. This made James and his advisor very suspicious.

James had advised the uncle of leaving some of the estate to his nephew. Understanding this case a little better now James could see why the uncle had provided in this way. Although this was not the wisest solution, obviously the uncle knew his nephew's character and he was not going to let this man spend his money that he had acquired by hard work and by economizing whenever needed.

What a lot of misery could have been prevented!

The nephew was well known in the business world. As a member of the Chamber of Commerce and the Country Club, he had status, but was he liked? His social situation was okay, but he was not exactly liked and nobody had looked into his business or his character so far.

James was advised to distance himself for a while from his law firm and keep a low profile. His colleagues believed in him and so did his family, but in such cases, the accused and everyone around him are victimized, guilty or not as the case may be, but the paparazzi had a victory for the moment.

Mark, as a Professor felt that he should be setting an example for the young students at the University and as long as there could be talk, he might be better off out of that situation for a while. Mark discussed this with the President of the U and he asked for a year's leave of absence and received this without any trouble.

He was also lucky to be able to step in as Concert Master with a part of the orchestra of the Vancouver Symphony, who were just going on a tour to Europe and probably Australia. The agent was just putting the final touches on the Down Under tour. Mark had been playing with the Symphony Orchestra now for several years.

For Mark and his position as Professor this worked out well, but he still had not seen Ashley and he had not been trying, thinking that she would know all about the debacle by now. She was on his mind though. This situation made for another two victims of the crime.

James and his father hired the best defense lawyer in Vancouver, who knew a first class investigator.

First of all they needed to know the background of the nephew as well as the uncle's relationship or rather his non-relationship with his deceased brother's son.

At first the detective had a hard time. He felt his questions were not being answered in a straight forward manner.

The first break through was at the Country Club, where he found that the nephew had a massive outstanding bill. After some routing around, he found that the nephew played too much poker and had lost a huge amount of money at the poker table.

Some members informed the investigator that his wife had left him taking their three children with her; they did not know where she and the children could be. She was demanding money to take care of her children. The separation had been kept very quiet, but it was now starting to leak out that not only was his wife not getting enough money to live decently with the children but she had been seen with bruises and an arm in a cast a while ago. People were starting to wonder! Mr. Clean did not look so clean now!

Slow but sure doors were being opened and people started to talk. It took a while to find the domicile of the wife with her children. She had moved to Osoyoos where her parents lived. They had arrived in her car but with very little clothing or toys and no money. Parents, wife and the children now too had become victims.

After sleuthing around some more the investigator found out that the husband had been gambling and drinking for several years. With the loss of money, the abuse had started. It was reported that the children had been afraid of their father for some time. The detective questioned the wife but she did not know much about her husband's business.

The lawyer and investigators had put out some careful feelers in the business direction and the result was not pretty. The investment business had been going down for quite a long time. The nephew had tried to fill the gap by borrowing from his uncle, who was not the lending kind. They found out that income tax had not been paid.

He tried to win money back by gambling, which obviously did not work. On the contrary he got deeper and deeper in debt, but he had always been convinced that he would inherit his uncle's money and estates, being the only surviving inheritor.

According to the employees the investigator discovered that there had been some really noisy quarrels in the uncle's office.

Uncovering all these leads to this crime took a lot of time. The nephew had succeeded in covering up his crimes for a long time and had done this very well so far.

Not inheriting his uncle's money had made him extremely angry and probably hopeless; he was ready to do anything to get to that lovely lolly. He now knew that the last quarrel with his relative had worsened his case, but he wanted that money so badly he decided to accuse the first man he could think of, his uncle's lawyer, who had brought him the news that he had inherited absolutely nothing.

He thought himself to be the victim! Did he care about his victims? According to him his wife was a wimp to run home when things became a little difficult. Did he not remember the beatings and the black eye he had given her lately? Or how rough he had been with their children? Was it their fault that he went gambling?

When would he learn that money is not everything?

Maybe in prison!

CHAPTER 6

Mark was often on her mind she missed him as well his conversations and opinions about music and general matters. She needed to learn to live with the situation even though she did not understand it. This was too hard to take. She loved Mark so much. She understood that now even better than before.

She was continuing her violin and piano studies, which she loved anyway, but she took it a little easier and did not take any other courses.

When she signed up for the violin course she heard that Dr. Maxwell was not teaching this year. After some inquiring she found that he was traveling in Europe with a part of the Vancouver Symphony as concertmaster and that this tour would probably extend to a tour in Australia. She knew then that she should definitely put Mark out of her head. This however was easier said than done.

Could she let her thoughts go where they should? Her mind relentlessly turned to Mark.

Ashley tried hard to forget Mark Maxwell by working as much as possible as every moment of free time brought automatically thoughts of him. By studying and teaching intensively, she tried to keep her thoughts away from him. She sometimes felt isolated and lonely. Then again what did she know about Mark and his family? Too many questions!

Basically all she knew and indeed this was important to

her, was his view on music and nature. To both Ashley and Mark this was most influential in their lives: music and nature interacting, inspiring, and giving new ideas for emotions in music and song. They had not talked about religion very much all they really knew was that they were both Catholic. But how far did that worship go? There had not been time to discuss those more intimate opinions and views.

From their conversations it showed that Mark loved his mother very much and was fond of his older brothers James and Sean. One thing she knew since he had severed ties with the U and left the country, was that things between her and Mark had definitely finished.

She threw herself into her schoolwork. She felt her music teaching should reach deeper into the feelings and emotions of her students. Most could now see how emotions or feelings are shown in music. Of course Ashley let the students listen to funny music as "Peter and the Wolf" by Prokofiev or a lullaby and just for fun she let them put their heads on the desk and showed them how they are lulled to sleep by the music.

She knew she could not reach everyone but most of them had chosen a certain instrument in which he or she wanted to excel. And with her guidance she hoped to succeed in helping her students reach their goal.

This year Ashley planned to enter competitions. With a lighter study load she could devote time to travel with her groups. As an extra-curricular activity these students at Grade 11 and 12 levels had joined either: the band and/or the more classical orchestra or the choir.

Sorting these young people's preferences and accomplishments had been quite an undertaking. Last year's students had of course already a good background. Ashley was now able to divide the students into their different sections.

She applied for several competitions with her groups. In January they started to compete with different schools in the city.

Ashley was so fortunate as to have volunteer help from parents in supervising the different classes when they traveled from school to school. These parents were so interested in their children's education and behavior as well as their musical performance. This does not happen too often.

So many parents and coaches push their children into sports. Ashley certainly encouraged plenty of sports, but only up to spending part of the student's time. There should be room for other activities as art and music. After all, art and music may be enjoyed for the rest of their lives.

They had a true homogeneous group with similar ideas and communication seemed to flow. However there is always something to dent the balloon and especially with teenagers. Nothing is accomplished until the end.

On one of these big performing days there was the bus in front of the school, loaded with the instruments. There were the parents, supervisors, Ashley and a few students. Everyone was becoming restless. Where were the others?

How anxious everyone was! What could have happened? Ashley had organized everything with lots of time to spare.

Finally a few students turned up and then a few more dribbled in and all were ready and eager to go. Why were they all so late?

From this charged up group came finally the unbelievable explanation. On the bulletin board the announcement of the bus leaving was at 10 a.m. Stupefied Ashley said: "I put the flyer with the departing time of 9 a.m. on myself."

Anyway this was not the time to sort out this puzzle and all left in the bus. They arrived with no time to spare. Though the band members had been upset at first they performed very well.

They played "Ode to Joy" by Beethoven and the choir sang Schiller's words: "All men shall be brothers."

The words fit in so beautifully with the music and the band did a fantastic job expressing the feelings of this magical piece. Ashley was just done in by the way her band and choir had performed this composition and she apparently was not the only one.

The adjudicator and committee gave the band and choir first prize for their performance of: "Ode to Joy".

The students were overjoyed. On their return in the bus they were noisy and boisterous, but Ashley and her supervisors really felt the same. Everyone was buoyed up. It was a wild group that returned to school. The principal congratulated them all and thought it smart to dismiss class until after lunch.

Was there no punishment for the prank that someone had played on the bulletin board?

No punishment by the principal was necessary as the band members let it be known that they were not slow in finding the immature culprit. His friends would ostracize him. For a teenager that must have been the worst punishment. Indeed he was quiet for a long time.

The band and choir performed this music again at the end of June, when they received a standing ovation from parents, friends and students.

One member of the band and one from the choir came up to the stage as representatives of the two groups, with an enormous bouquet for Miss Van Heekeren, who had led them to the top of High School music performers in the city.

Of course Ashley's family and their friend Uncle Peter attended the concert too. They were so happy for her.

The sad part of this occasion was that most of the music students were leaving school and less than half would be returning and become Grade 12 students in the fall. But as is usual for teachers it was a wrench to part, but a challenge to start the new year in September with the former Grade 11 students, now Grade 12 and the new Grade 11 students for band and choir. The usual music classes in Grade 9 and 10 were the starters for band and choir.

CHAPTER 7

Mark enjoyed his playing with the orchestra and the traveling from city to city in Europe. They usually spent several days in a city rehearsing and trying out a new program. Of course the violin study was there for him every day. He also visited many areas in the different countries in which they performed. He saw striking landscapes and interesting views as the flat lands and waterways in Holland with its many windmills and canals all around. The beautiful structured old buildings attached to each other. The gables were all different heights and design. Holland's marvelous evening skies were an inspiration for him. He loved the area in southern France and revisited the fields and castles south west of Paris.

Like a painter who grabs his brush, Mark, picked up his violin. Occasionally when the music inspired him he composed a song. Sometimes when thinking of Ashley, his mind became somber and his music gloomy.

After the New Year, the orchestra moved to Sydney and played in that wonderful music hall, where the acoustics were so exceptional. The building of this concert hall had taken many years. It was situated at the water's edge. The architecture of that building with the harbor as background was so stimulating for an artist like Mark. From there they traveled to Melbourne, Adelaide, Brisbane, and Perth.

All through his travels through Europe he felt lonely. Had

he done the right thing, leaving Ashley without saying anything?? How he would have loved showing Ashley Holland and Belgium, Paris and Italy. How they would have discussed what they saw and heard and felt. But he needed to be strong and stay away to evade any difficulty and embarrassment regarding his brother's court case, which at first did not look good at all.

The nephew had brought in all the big guns, which was a good start for him. So many lawyers had swindled their clients before, which had given the profession such a bad name.

All the proofs of innocence had to come from James's side and at first that did not look too good. His accountant showed the books, which according to the Defense lawyer seemed okay, but James could have stashed the money elsewhere.

The detective that James' lawyer had hired, had to work pretty carefully and diplomatically so as not to raise any suspicions. Through the grapevine they obtained connections of the nephew to people that were willing to spill the beans. They had to inquire into his business and personal bank accounts. They found the wife's bank account was very minimal, which showed that the nephew either had no moneys or that he did not care a fig about his wife's comfort. Maybe both!!

There finally came a little light at the end of the tunnel, when one of the nephew's office assistants, who felt he had been slighted by his boss, mentioned not only the slow paying of salaries in the office, but also offered a few names of lenders and banks that had been snooping around the building.

These contacts were approached and they did not make a pretty picture. After quite an amount of time one gambling outfit after the other came to light.

The investigator followed the nephew at night and saw him entering a normal looking building. After a few minutes the detective rang the bell of this same building and was asked what his business was. He had to find a quick excuse and asked to see Mr. John Smith.

While the porter checked the names on the board, the investigator looked over the porter's shoulder and noticed some names of high-ranking people on the board, as well as the nephew's name.

The porter said: "Mr. John Smith is not here yet, but you could leave your name here and he may phone you."

The investigator promised to phone the "phony" Mr. Smith. He had seen and heard enough. He could hear the poker chips rustling. He knew now in what kind of circles he could go for more information regarding this gambling outfit.

As there were names of well-known lawyers on the board, he thought it best to tell his boss, James' lawyer about this, who again via friends, got the info that the nephew was indeed a member of this club and owed thousands of dollars to other members and lenders.

He also found out that the nephew was a member of two more clandestine gambling outfits and owed thousands of dollars there too.

Now the authorities could get involved. These matters were looked at officially and the enquiry showed that the nephew had swindled plenty of company money and also had mortgaged his house and office building to the hilt. His income tax had not been paid for this year, and they found last year's declaration was questionable. Many secrets were now uncovered.

There was the broken marriage and the nephew had apparently had illicit affairs as well. No wonder that his wife wanted out!

James turned the table and sued the nephew for defamation of character. Not only his reputation had been attacked but also his law business had been put on hold by this malicious libel.

As things move rather slowly in the courts it took many

more months to get back to normal. But would it come back to normal for all the victims?

For James and his wife it was a slow return to their previous way of living.

For the nephew's wife and children it would take a very long time to get used to living without husband and father. With the help of her parents the wife might be able to make a living in her former profession as a nurse. She would need to upgrade her qualifications, which costs time and money, while the children at first were looked after by the wife's parents. Later that too had to be sorted out.

Ashley still did not know anything about this court case. She was too busy attempting to forget Mark and trying the best she could do with her teaching of music and her own studies. Colette and Andrew could see that she was not her former happy self. As she was rather a loner, she did not talk much with others at the University and certainly not about Dr. Mark.

When her parents asked what was wrong, she said: "Mom, Dad my trouble will resolve itself with time."

Her parents kept up to date with the case and also knew that Mark's brother James had been exonerated, but they had not told their daughter because they did not want to cause anymore pain as she never wanted to talk about Mark. They thought to leave this information to Mark. They heard through acquaintances in the music world that the Vancouver Symphony's concerts in Europe and later in Australia were very well attended. Its conductor had to fly home for a while due to sickness and Mark took over the baton. Under Mark's direction they changed the program a tiny little bit, in agreement with the orchestra, by including some foot tapping music as an encore, which went off very well.

The art section of the papers in Europe reported the success of the Vancouver Symphony several times.

Upon his return the official conductor pointed out that he

appreciated what Mark had done for the orchestra, by putting on his own stamp on it. He wanted to continue this program. Mark and he became even better friends and they worked together on performing well-known or more popular music. The younger public as well as the older generation seemed to appreciate this kind of music. The orchestra had tried this out in Australia with a huge success.

Mark was to take up his former position at UBC as Professor of Music, and he played regularly as Concertmaster with the Vancouver Symphony. In case of absence of the official conductor, Mark would take over the baton.

The planning committee of this orchestra was taken in by Mark's choices of music as well as his manner of directing while playing his beloved violin.

For this season they would play a mixture of the lighter happier music and the beautiful emotional classics for two of the six upcoming concerts.

Mark had returned to Vancouver for the start of the new school year at UBC. His thoughts were never far away from Ashley, but now since his family's troubles were straightened out and he was back again in Vancouver, Mark wanted to see her. Would she want to see him? He doubted this but he would try and eventually try again.

It was easy enough to find out where she was at the U. What classes was she taking? The secretaries were willing enough to help this friendly good-looking prof. She was taking again a Saturday morning class in Music appreciation and therapy.

He thought he would find her in the cafeteria after classes, but he had gambled wrongly. Ever since he had dropped contact with Ashley, she had been going home.

He was disappointed, but he would try again next week and be at her class's exit. Indeed he saw her, but she was so busy talking to a friend and a male at that! Mark did not feel too good about that and on top of it he was sure that she had seen him and looked right through him and then away as she left with that fellow.

Mark felt slighted and hurt. Was this jealousy? But later on he thought he should try to see her again and be firmer this time. After all he thought this young immature looking fellow would be no good for Ashley and maybe there were no feelings involved. Perhaps he had been too hasty.

Ashley had indeed seen him and was really shocked but a year's absence had made her stronger. She had not shown any expression on her face and was extremely friendly to her student friend. She was convinced that he would not try to see her again.

However the next Saturday he was a little sneakier. He had been standing against the wall so she could not see him, and he surprised her totally. Mark took her by the hand and led her to the cafeteria. She tried to escape at first, but he just smiled at her (which was her undoing). He said: "Come along please, I need to talk to you."

She chided herself later about this: weak-kneed and all, she said to herself I can at least hear what he has to say for himself.

They found a quiet spot. He asked her how she was and of course she said: "OK." She was not going to tell him how hurt and shocked she had been and actually still was, for the wound in her heart had not healed.

When she did not say anything and seemed to wait for his opening, he said: "You heard and read about my family's scandal?"

She surprised him then when she said: "What scandal?" She tried to explain that she had been so busy with her studies and teaching and had very little time for anything else, let alone reading newspapers. She did not mention the little fact that she had tried hard to forget him by working as much as possible.

Mark explained what had happened and that he had

thought it was better for her and her family not to be involved with the court case, because if the papers would have heard of a connection between the two families, they would have stressed the story and maybe would have included your father being a lawyer in the Federal government in this scandal.

Ashley mentioned the fact that they were supposed to be friends and as friends they could probably have helped each other. She said: "I just don't understand that you left without a word, never wrote or phoned! What was I to think? Right now I want to go home and think about this a little bit."

Upon this she stood up and went home, leaving him standing astonished and helpless. He did not understand this situation. With his male attitude he could only think that he had apologized and explained everything. That's all. Case closed.

Mark still had a lot to learn.

When Ashley got to her car she managed to drive to the park and in a quiet spot she had a good howl. She thought that she had got over her feelings for Mark. What was the matter with her? And she had made up her mind not to fall in love with anyone again so easily. This experience had hurt too much. She would just have to go on living but without Mark on her mind. This was easier said than done.

Of course Andrew and Colette noticed immediately that something was wrong with their daughter, but they left her alone for a while to give her time to recuperate.

After supper when Tom had gone out and Ashley was left alone with her parents, Colette asked her to tell them what was wrong. Maybe they could help.

Ashley told them what had happened these last two Saturdays and she also reiterated that if you want to be friends you should be able to talk about all your troubles. And I even thought we were more than "friends".

Then Andrew said: "Maybe we were wrong too. We noticed that you didn't know what was happening in the Maxwell family. We thought that if Mark wanted to keep quiet about the scandal, it was his prerogative to do so. The tabloids really used a lot of slander. The papers made money. And who cares about the disgrace to victims and family of victims and even friends of victims? The paparazzi had a hay day; they can say whatever they like without any proof and what is the reader to know? You can be sure that Mark's father and the brothers both being in the law business suffered from this. Mother Maxwell as a pediatrician was so very much needed and therefore her job was not in danger. And you seemed to be settling down after a while (a stiff upper lip, we presumed). You had a lot of work to worry about at that time. Maybe now you can see things more clearly and look at what has been done to Mark and his family. Mark probably thought that he could hide from this malignancy by fleeing to Europe or he had other reasons as well. Who knows? He probably wants to tell you about that."

Mark too thought this situation over and planned to see Ashley again the next Saturday. He knew now that his feelings for her went deeper than he had thought while he was away, because Mark had found in Ashley a combination of intelligence and sensuality and beauty and most of all love. While he was in Europe he had wondered about her, but his thoughts were being kept so busy with his family's trouble and this music tour, especially when he had to take over the conducting during the time that the actual conductor became ill.

And now that he had seen her, he knew that he truly loved her. He made up his mind; he was going to see her again and take her out for lunch if that was possible. He would explain the whole case. He planned to do everything possible to get her back.

First he would have to get her to come with him after class.

Saturday came and Mark was ready. He had his arm around her waist before she knew what was happening. He drew her along and explained that he wanted to take her out for lunch to a quiet place and talk with her.

She came along with him this time. Mark took her to a nice quiet restaurant and only after they had ordered from the menu, did they discuss their difficulties. Mark told her straight away that he cared for her and the nine months of traveling had not changed his feelings and regards for her. On the contrary Ashley was always on his mind. He explained the difficulties in his family, but now these were clearing up. His brother James had been proven innocent, and the criminal would be imprisoned for a long time to come. He also told her about the battered wife and children.

Ashley could see that Mark felt deeply involved in his family's trouble and she could understand and appreciate that. She would have had the same feelings if anything like this had happened to her family.

But as she told Mark she still could not see why he had not told her about this before he left for Europe. He had said himself he wanted friendship, but what are friends for if not at least to listen to their friend's troubles.

Mark answered: "I am sorry that I did not see it that way at the time, but I thought you would know about the case and then understand. I can see now where my lack of communication led to and why you doubt me now.

Ashley said: "But even if I had known the situation, what difference would that have made? You did not tell me anything, you just left and I repeat: friends discuss their troubles. Communication helps so much in time of trouble."

Mark touched her hand, looked into her eyes and asked her to begin their friendship again and get to know and understand each other a lot better.

He saw her doubts in her face and her uncertainty in their friendship. He finally started to comprehend the shock Ashley had suffered and her doubt in their "friendship" when he so suddenly had not contacted her anymore. He then suggested dinner with his parents and brothers that night. He told her they went out to eat every Saturday night to a different restaurant and this time it would be Chinese. He hoped that she would see and understand how close-knit his family was. Ashley agreed; but she wondered later on whether she had done the right thing to meet the Maxwell family. She knew she loved Mark, but she also realized that in a relationship communication and commitment were needed just as she saw in her own parents' marriage. There was love and friendship, exchange of ideas and opinions. Well, she would see what her ideas and feelings would be after the night was over.

Ashley told her parents what had happened. They agreed with her to go slowly in this relationship even though they could have seen difficulties if Mark's brother had lost his case.

Six o'clock came near and Ashley was dressed and her face made up. She was lovely her parents thought. But how did she feel?

Mark came in just long enough to greet Colette and Andrew, but he could not keep his eyes off Ashley. "Wow", he said. "Do you look beautiful! That blue-nearly purplish color of your dress matches your eyes."

Once they were in the car Mark noticed that Ashley was very quiet. There were so many thoughts warring inside her head. She knew she loved Mark but so far he had disappointed her so much. Again she asked herself if he cannot discuss important matters now how will that go later on.

She wanted to be sure of him. She needed his trust and friendship as well as his love. She felt that communication was absolutely important in marriage and that was what Ashley actually hoped for. She knew that she loved, actually adored Mark.

"My parents won't eat you and James and Sean will be having a wonderful time telling their jokes and funny stories and their wives too are wonderful people." he said.

The family had arrived and introductions were made. They had a glass of wine first to loosen up the tongues. And indeed after a few minutes conversation flowed easier.

Father Maxwell asked if Ashley had any preferences in Chinese food. She said she liked most dishes, but to her the best was spicy General Chow's chicken.

All the dishes were set out on a large lazy Susan in the middle of the table and every one helped themselves to the food.

The atmosphere at the table was buoyant. Ashley was sitting between Mark and Sean and Allyson with Mr. and Mrs. Maxwell across the table and James and his wife Marlese occupied the seats at the end of the table.

Ashley liked Mark's mother immediately. She was a good-looking quiet spoken woman, who seemed to be very much loved by her husband and three sons, who teased her a lot. They called her *Mrs. Baby-doctor.*

She explained she had stopped working until her three babies weren't babies anymore. She had gone back to work when Mark, the youngest went to school. She told Ashley that he was not an easy little child unless he heard music. One day they had taken him to Sean's school band performance. He not only loved the music, but while dancing up and down, he said: "I want to play that" and pointed to the violin.

Mark's mother got some information from Sean's music teacher about violins for a tot like Mark and he might be able to find a violin teacher for him. No one in their family was musical. They just enjoyed good music.

Mark's birthday was coming up and what better than to give him a small violin, suitable for him.

From then on there was no difficult, bored little boy anymore. His teacher said he was a natural. He was astonished what sound that small child could get out of that child sized violin.

Of course now he had to study scales, but even that did

not give as much trouble as they had expected once he saw the reason for the practice. Everyone thought that he would soon give this instrument up and would want to play with other children. He might play for a while, then he came back again to his own little music world.

Ashley enjoyed hearing about Mark's childhood. They all seemed to get along so well and the Chinese food was delicious. The brothers joked and teased their sibling about his violin, which was like a blanket to other children. They told her he brought that thing wherever he went. The parents had to ban the violin from the bathroom.

When Mark brought her home, he asked if Ashley would like to do this again next week and though Ashley beforehand had made up her mind to keep the relationship in slow motion, she agreed to have dinner with the Maxwell family next Saturday night. Mark seemed very pleased about this. He brought Ashley home and asked her if she would have lunch with him on Saturday as they used to do. Ashley agreed to meet him at the cafeteria.

When Andrew and Colette came home that night from a play they had attended at the theatre down town, Ashley told them where she had been and how much she had enjoyed Mark's family. Andrew had met Judge Maxwell at several meetings he said and had found him very agreeable.

Ashley also described the two brothers and how they poked fun at their "baby" brother. She told her parents that she would go for dinner with them next Saturday.

Colette could now see where things were going and she suggested that Mark could come for dinner the following Sunday, that is if Ashley would like that.

The next week the two of them were practically back to where they had left off a year ago or rather there seemed to be a little more communication from Mark's side. He opened up more on his opinions with regard to religion, morals and of course music was never far out of their conversation.

During the week they did not see much of each other. Mark was teaching and evenings were for studying his violin and rehearsing with the orchestra. There always seemed to be meetings either for Mark or for Ashley. Ashley had her teaching and much of her extra time was spent on the school band. It had now become a habit to have lunch with Mark on Saturday after her class at the U, supper with the Maxwell family and Sunday dinner with the Van Heekeren bunch.

They started to feel that they did not see enough of each other. Ashley was still living at home as did Tom, her brother. Tom was finishing off his Master's degree in Architecture. Mark being older had moved out of the family home a while ago and rented a pleasant apartment in easy reach of UBC as well as the concert hall downtown.

His parents had a wonderful large house in West Vancouver on Marine Drive, but Mark was wasting too much time traveling. He missed however the view of the water with its large freighters and at night the fairy-like view of all the boats and cruise ships lit up, but he also needed his independence.

Their friendship had been growing and had grown into "loving." They had come to the point of kissing and touching each other more intimately and they knew they should not go any further. Mark wanted to go farther in their relationship and they talked about making a commitment and getting engaged.

Ashley discussed this with her parents. What about an engagement party around Christmas time and the wedding either at Easter holidays or the end of June after school was finished? Ashley would not take a class for her doctoral degree that summer, so that they could have a good long holiday together.

Mark's apartment was not really suitable for their needs, for their ambitions, instruments and books they had to have ample room. Mark had done well financially and invested well. He thought they should start looking for a nice house in a good locality within easy reach of the U., where they could eventually bring up a family.

Their engagement party went off as they had dreamed with a catered dinner at the Maxwell's house. The whole family was present; grandfather Maxwell as well as Ashley's grandparents, who had arrived from The Hague a few days earlier. They celebrated Christmas and engagement all in one big party.

Ashley and Mark were so happy. They started looking for a house on Saturdays after they had had their lunch. Sometimes Mark would see a house in the evening if there was a chance, but it took them four Saturdays and several Real Estate agents before they saw this older house as they had more or less seen in their imagination. It was in a quiet street with large trees on both sides, not far from the University and only one bus ride away from Ashley's school. It was one block away from the coast. It had a lovely, good-sized garden, which was important to them, especially for later when they would have children. The children would need to play there and feel free and protected. There were large trees at the end of the yard, giving possibilities for a tree house, or camping in the garden later on.

The house was roomy with a large living room opening up through French doors onto a flagged stone patio and a view of the garden that was fenced in by a hedge all around, giving privacy.

Mark had a stand-up piano but they dreamed of a grand piano later on. They already knew the exact place for this instrument in the spacious living room.

There were two bedrooms down stairs; one with an ensuite, the other one would be lovely for Mark's study. It was large enough to have a desk in it for Ashley if they wanted to work together. This room was going to be sound proofed giving Mark a chance for playing and composing without being disturbed by outside noises. That way no one would need to be afraid to make too much noise or trouble for Mark, especially with some rambunctious kiddies in the house eventually.

There were three bedrooms upstairs, but for the time being they would only use the master bedroom. The next day both sets of parents came over to see their find, they all thought that the house was suitable and they should put a bid in.

Mark's free time was stretched to the limit running from Real Estate to Bank to lawyer. He was able to get the house and move in just before Easter, which would give him a chance to organize the house during the holidays and settle in.

Everyone promised to help. There were Mark's two brothers and Tom, Ashley's brother. They all had strong backs. Now Mark and Ashley just had to wait for Easter to come.

CHAPTER 8

February 2nd was a most miserable day. There was a foreboding gloom in the air on this dismal cold cloudy day. It had been sleeting rain all day and it was freezing. It felt like it might snow any minute. Everyone tried to get home and stay warm near a fire place.

Colette and Andrew were tired and went to bed early while Ashley was going to finish off some work in her room. They left the lights on downstairs for Tom. He was working late with a friend on a mutual project for their studies and he had warned his parents that he would be home late, as they wanted to finish a certain part of the project that night. They could go to bed without worrying about Tom's coming home so late.

A little after eleven p.m. the bell rang. Ashley thought, Oh Tom you must have forgotten your keys.

Ashley tripped downstairs saying: "Hey bro, do you have to wake us all up?"Opening the door for Tom, did she get a surprise! There was no Tom to tease, but a young serious looking RCMP officer, who explained that he was right around the corner when the message came about Tom Van Heekeren, who had had an accident. Ashley said: "Yes, that's my brother. What is wrong?"

He answered: "Your brother Tom has had a serious accident and is in the hospital. If you want to come with me that would be faster."

Ashley said: "Please come in while I get my parents."

Andrew and Colette had heard the noise and jumped into some clothes and were already coming down the stairs. They had heard the last part of what the policeman had said about the accident. Colette grabbed her purse and they all got into the police car. The officer drove at a terrific speed, which he could do being the police. He told them he didn't know exactly what had happened, but he had heard about it on his radio and as he was so close, he got orders to go to the house and bring them the bad news. He told them that he had gone to High School with Tom.

Upon arriving at the emergency they were told to come right through and there was Tom. His head injury was extremely bad, the Doctor said.

Tom opened his eyes and said: "Bye Mom, Dad, I love you."

Colette kissed him and made a cross on his forehead. Andrew and Ashley kissed him too. Then he closed his eyes and was gone.

The Doctor confirmed his death.

They stayed for a few minutes and prayed for his soul.

They took a cab to the police station. The police told them that on the icy street Tom's car had slipped and wrapped itself around the electric pole. The car itself was badly damaged, but it was repairable. If it was not for the unfortunate bad hit on the head, Tom might have lived.

Parents and sister went home. Ashley gave her Mom and Dad a stiff brandy and they all made the motion of going to bed for the few hours that were left of the night. Colette and Andrew held on to each other. They still could not fathom that Tom would not come home anymore. Colette had never seen Andrew cry and she thought she would never see anything worse than seeing her beloved Andrew crying and sobbing. They were lying there holding on to each other until daylight came and they knew that they had to get up and face the world. They had to organize the funeral and let people know about Tom's death.

Ashley, though she was terribly upset, did most of the phoning, but Andrew and Colette had to take care of a certain amount themselves. The three of them sat together crying softly.

The schools were generous and told Colette not to come to school for a week.

Ashley phoned Mark, who came over as soon as possible. Mark held Ashley until she could finish sobbing.

A lawyer friend, Brian Montgomery, would take care of meetings with police, car insurance and Tom's life insurance.

Many attended the funeral. Several priests from Tom's High School celebrated the Eucharist. His friends and profs from the U were there as well as Mark's family. And of course Andrew's and Colette's family and friends came to the funeral. At the reception every one told Colette and Andrew what a great man Tom had been and what his friendship had meant to them. Every one told them of some good experience with Tom and how well regarded he was. Tom's death had been a shock to all who knew him.

His profs observed that with Tom's passing many architectural ideas and art were lost. They maintained that he would have had a great future.

The president of the architectural firm where Tom had worked remarked that Tom's death also meant a great loss for him as well as the firm. Tom's creativity was outstanding and several of his ideas had been used by the firm. "This is exceptional," the speaker said "for such a young man."

A few days after the funeral, Andrew's friend Brian came over and told him that there was trouble with the Insurance Company. They were trying to prove that Tom had been intoxicated, which meant that the double indemnity of the insurance policy was not valid. Andrew could not believe what he heard. Tom only had an occasional glass of wine with his meal. Brian went to see Tom's friend where he had spent the night of the accident. The friend's parents too vouched that the boys had been working on their project and the friend showed Brian what they had been doing that night.

Could Tom have gone to the bar after working with Brian? He had left his friend's house at 10:45 and the RCMP was at Tom's house at 11 o'clock.

If it were not such a serious case, it would have been a totally laughable idea. Brian got in contact with the Police and Doctors, but no one had noticed any smell of alcohol anywhere.

What Brian did not tell the Van Heekerens at first was that the insurance agent had offered him half the indemnity if he could help prove that there was alcohol involved. Brian thought Andrew had suffered enough. He let the whole case settle down first before he mentioned this fraud to Andrew.

Several weeks later when the insurance money was paid out Brian told the Van Heekerens this story and advised them to take another more honest insurance company.

The Van Heekeren's house was so quiet now. Every one tried to put their thoughts to their work. Tom's liveliness was missed so much. Ashley thought she would have loved to open the door for Tom even at 3 a.m.

Colette was sitting at her desk one night, thinking about Tom and wrote the following:

Our Son

You left us much too early
You needed to accomplish so much yet
But the Lord needed you more.

Now you look down upon us
With your lovely smile.

We know in our hearts
That you are in a better place.

No sorrows or pains
Still we wanted to keep you here.

Like the soaring eagle
Watching us from up high
You'll be keeping an eye on your loved ones.

Your dreams and thoughts have stopped
But we will remember your thoughtfulness.

We pray that the Lord may give his unerring love
To those you left on this earth.

May the Lord let Peace
Flow over us and heal our hearts.

Mark came over as often as he could to cheer up Ashley and her parents. At first they would not go out even to visit friends. Peter came and tried to take them out or asked them for supper at his apartment. They felt frozen; nothing had a meaning to the parents. But life had to go on.

Finally the Maxwells talked them into coming over for

Sunday dinner. This went off well. They knew in their hearts they had to start living again. They had practically thrown themselves into their work

However Colette found it too hard to work on her book; the creative juices were not running. She just could not think or write, hopefully she could come back to this later. She needed the liveliness of her pupils and the thoughtfulness of her colleagues and she needed Andrew more than ever; just as Andrew needed all Colette's attention and love.

They now also thought of Ashley who was grieving too and for her they should put up a good front.

Mark took possession of the house on March 15th and had cleaners take care of the initial cleaning. Neither he nor Ashley had much energy left. They had got behind in their work and study. They knew that it was best for them to work hard to keep the tragedy a little away from their minds.

Ashley helped Mark Saturdays, after her class at the U, to set up the house. She took care of the kitchen and Mark tried to organize his office as one of the first things to make the house livable.

After a few weeks Ashley joined the Maxwell family again for Saturday dinner. She needed the upbeat atmosphere of the three brothers. At first she felt guilty leaving her parents, but they practically pushed her out of the house and told her to get a life.

The two lovers decided to postpone their marriage until July or August. They would discuss this with the parents again. Anyway they now wanted a very small simple wedding. It would be hard for them to wait so long, but they did not feel that they could have a celebration as early as Easter as they had planned. It was too soon after the tragic accident. Especially Colette's and Andrew's minds were not geared for celebrating.

For the time being they would put the house in order and

Mark would move in. He just closed the doors of the rooms he would not be using.

Ashley had to study for her exam, which was not so easy to do after the death of her beloved brother. But nothing would bring him back! With her parents' encouragement she managed to study hard and pass her exam.

The Van Heekeren's house seemed so silent and empty. Not only happy-go-lucky Tom had left, but also Ashley would soon fly the coup. Andrew and Colette had ideas of moving to a smaller place, but they decided not to do anything until after the wedding; that would give them time to think and look around for an apartment.

In the meantime plans had to be made for the wedding. They decided on July 15th. That would give them time to finish off their school year, organize the house and keep up with their lovely garden, with its colorful bushes of rhododendrons and hydrangeas. These bushes need constant trimming of old flowers and the different kinds of roses were so beautiful. Even when it was raining or there was a dull day as it so often is in Vancouver, the colorful splashes of these flowers were bright and stimulating. Both young people put in a lot of time in this garden. Once the holidays started Colette came over to give them a helping hand.

Every time a trip to the new house was made there was a carload of stuff that Ashley had collected and the wedding presents started to come in. The students gave Ashley a surprise party; as did her colleagues.

Plans for the next school year had to be made. Ashley had to take one more course and to write her dissertation for her Ph.D. Quite an amount of research had been done already in preparation as she knew all along what she wanted to research and prove. In this she had Mark's full attention as his thoughts went into the same direction as Ashley's ideas about music.

Music was so important in their lives. Music enjoyment and appreciation could be brought to many people. But not just one kind of music! There is so much out there for everyone to enjoy; from jazz, rock, to light music, pop, or classical. Each kind of music has an influence on different people, just as the impact from a person's culture and background affects each person.

Colette used to tell the story of her musical education where her mother each morning switched on the radio, put the program for her daughter to follow beside her plate. There used to be a classical program from 8 - 9 a.m. Thus Colette was practically indoctrinated with the masterpieces of Tchaikovsky, Brahms, Bach, Beethoven, and Berlioz. Then there were the piano studies each day for half an hour immediately after school.

But for now: first the wedding and the moving had to be arranged. July 15th was coming up fast; though not exactly for Mark and Ashley who did not find it so easy not to touch each other so intimately. All their grieving for Tom had not eradicated their intense love for each other. On the contrary! They needed each other even more.

Slow but sure Colette and Andrew forced themselves to get into the mood of their daughter's wedding. They helped out where they could.

CHAPTER 9

Finally the wedding day arrived. Ashley was leaving her home, which was so hard to take especially for her father. Was there a man good enough for his beautiful darling daughter?

Both parents walked down the aisle with her in the wonderfully, decorated church, where Mark was waiting at the front of the church.

He turned at the first strains of the music and was bowled over by the beauty of his bride. Her curly light blond hair peeped out from around the veil.

Nearing the altar Ashley saw the loving look of admiration on her, so soon to be husband. She then felt sure and satisfied to go into this union with Mark. Both parents noticed the high regard and affection this young couple showed towards each other and felt at peace and assured.

Though the festivities were kept to a minimum the church celebration was exceptional with the full choir and Symphony orchestra in deference of their concert-master Dr. Mark Maxwell.

Sean's and Allyson's little girls were the most beautiful bride's maids. They felt so proud of themselves carrying the rings to the altar. Afterwards, Ashley told them what a wonderful job they had done.

The church was packed; outside were many of Mark's and

Ashley's students, who had come to see their favorite teachers and congratulate them.

From the church the family of Mark and Ashley all went to the Vancouver hotel for an extensive lunch and reception.

The young married couple left late in the afternoon for a night flight to Fiji where they would spend their honeymoon and a well-deserved rest.

They truly enjoyed each other. They finally belonged together. They were convinced about their love, friendship and commitment. They would be happy together.

They loved the heat of the tropics and the scenery, but most of all the light- heartedness of the people. They all greet each other so happily, even strangers and as they say there, "Once you have said "hello" you are strangers no more."

While they were in Nadi they traveled by taxi to Suva visiting Pacific Harbor. They visited the Hindu Sri Siva Temple; saw the Meke, which is a mixture of dance, song and theatre. They heard and enjoyed Indian music and of course they had to see the Fijian Fire walking, which was accompanied by a Fijian orchestra.

All this traveling was done by taxi and they had the same driver every day. They got to know him very well. He taught them much about the island and its people, the habits and local foods. He brought them to different ethnic restaurants, where they ate taro, paw-paw, which is papaya, and roti an Indian kind of bread. There was not much that didn't taste good to them.

They visited the Hibiscus festival and the handicraft markets where the making of tapa cloth was shown. It is made from bark of the mulberry tree, soaked and pounded flat. After it is dried, rhythmic, geometric patterns are painted on the sheets of flattened and pounded bark.

But most enjoyable for them was their romp in their hotel room, where they enjoyed each other and got to know each other. It had been a long wait for them. However their respect and friendship for each other had paid off with their desire and love.

Both Mark and Ashley enjoyed scuba diving and Mark liked surfing. Of course they were very interested in Fijian musical instruments as the: Nose flute and other types of flutes made of bamboo, the dowlah, a kind of drum, an Indian percussion instrument and tabla drums. They loved the "dhola hindi" which is Indian folk music.

Mark and Ashley bought some bamboo flutes and tried them out, which gave the members of the hotel orchestra lots of amusement. They were asked to play along with them when they noticed how musical Mark was. Mark told them then that he played with the Vancouver Symphony orchestra.

The next evening Mark came in with his violin and he was asked to accompany them. They had a few try-outs. Then they all played together and had lots of fun. Ashley who taught recorder and flute at school played along too on her new bamboo flute.

The musicians told them they had never had so much pleasure as they had while playing with them. And of course this young musical couple had enjoyed playing as much with the orchestra. It certainly had been a wonderful experience for them, which they could use in their teaching and composing. On top of it all it had given them a new outlook on life. That's what the Fijians know how to do: have fun, be happy and laugh.

While in Fiji, Mark composed some short pieces of music with a Fijian influence.

On a different level these musicians had so much in common with Mark. With all the pleasure they had in performing they were totally enrapt in the music, just as Mark was when he was playing emotional or soul-stirring music. Mark experienced the cheerful, euphoric and rhythmic side of music. He mentioned later on that it feels as if the different instruments talk to each other and bring a conversation into the concert.

As Ashley had noticed so long ago when Mark had first played in one of her classes, he was so totally in the music and his way of playing was simply brilliant. She understood him when he said: "Put your soul into it."

She knew that when he played he was totally inspired by the sound of the music. While she observed all this, Ashley thought a person's imagination can take him or her anywhere, from a lovely tropical island beach setting with palms and flowers to a romantic gondola tour. Sometimes the words of the song are so impressive, another time the moving melody may inspire poetry.

One time Ashley noticed an old man in the crowd, who appeared to be so done in by the melody that a tear was rolling down his cheek.

As a "thank you" for having the same taxi-driver for the two weeks, the driver asked them to have dinner at his house. Mark and Ashley were surprised and pleased. They met the driver's wife, Mary, who was Indian and Catholic. She told them that she was brought up in a convent in Bombay. She was devoted to the Holy Mary as there were several paintings and statues of her in the house.

The driver said: "You are surprised that she is Catholic and I am Muslim."

Then he said jokingly: "I don't understand her religion but that doesn't bother us. We respect each other and allow each other the freedom of religions."

To Mark and Ashley they seemed to be quite happy in this relationship. The driver's wife was excited to have them over for dinner, which consisted of three different kinds of fish and veggies. Mary was so proud of her house, which was made of corrugated metal and painted bright blue, inside as well as outside. It certainly was different!

What a wonderful ending to their honeymoon. They took

home all these experiences and often talked about them afterwards.

While the young couple was away in Fiji and Andrew was working in the office, Colette was alone at home and was not so happy. Now both her beloved children were out of the house. It was so quiet. Andrew noticed Colette's unhappiness and often asked her to come downtown and have lunch with him or with some friends. He just wanted her mind to be occupied with happier thoughts, even though he too was still suffering from the loss of his wonderful son. This loss was certainly like a long good-bye, a very long good-bye.

Colette came home after a lunch and suddenly said to herself: "How can I complain? I still have the most loving husband, a job that I love a beautiful and now a so happy and accomplished daughter, who has given me so much love. And there is all this beautiful music I can play and listen to. God is taking good care of Tommy and all of us. I am actually rich."

From then on things went smoother. With Colette trying harder not to seem so depressed, Andrew too felt better. He had actually been hiding in his office. He now took a week's holiday during which time they gardened, went for long walks in Stanley Park or had a lovely dinner out.

Mark and Ashley still had a month of holidays before they would start their regular teaching session in September. They spent this time preparing their schoolwork and socializing, which was something they would not have much time for once they were teaching.

Colette and Andrew came over or the young couple would go to Ashley's parents place for a meal, or the Maxwells asked Mark, Ashley and her parents over for a leisurely dinner.

Colette had started writing again, which made her feel so much better. Since her association with her agent she had found success in publishing her story. She had nearly finished her new children's book. The first proof of the illustrations had just arrived. She showed them to Ashley and Mark.

Mark's head being always filled with music said: "Colette, could I have a copy of this? I think I have an idea."

Upon coming home he immediately started to read Colette's manuscript and he absorbed the writing. With the words in front of him he played a melody on the piano and mentioned to Ashley: "Your Mom's writing is fantastic. It does not only have a lovely rhythm and style, but the story too is so interesting. I think I can put this to music. This could be a children's CD to be followed along with the book Look what a combination and experience for a child, there are these lovely pictures, reading and music all in one or separate whatever the choice."

The story was about the Fair and fireworks. The music Mark made to go along was happy and exciting as fairs are and thunderous and rhythmic as fireworks can be. There was also a little Fijian influence making it more interesting. Listening to that music made her feet dance. Ashley took her bamboo flute and accompanied Mark.

THE FAIR

Fairy tale wonderland
What a wonderful world
Stars spattered all over the sky
Like fairy lights tumbling from up high.

Illuminated mystic ghosts and haunted castles
Magic power of the wonder-worker
Whizzing away the glimmering, twinkling lights
Laughing children twirling.

Along the boardwalk Aladdin
Plays his silver flute
Turning seniors young again
By his magic lute.

The barrel organ plays happy music
Serenading the crowd
With pulsing throbbing rhythm
Resonating and harmonizing.

Darkness falls
Foreboding the end of celebrations
Lights are extinguished
The end of a fabulous day!!

When Colette discovered what her son-in-law had done to the poem in her book she had tears in her eyes.

To a writer her book is like a child to her. Colette felt proud and happy as well as encouraged. She would get in touch with her agent. She wondered what he would say.

Andrew was so happy for his dear wife. This was just the uplift she needed after being so depressed since Tom's death.

And it did Andrew a world of good to see his wife so chipper.

The writing now would keep her mind so occupied, which again encouraged her to write more and more.

Mark and Ashley too were so excited about this, especially when they saw what good this was doing to Colette.

It took a good two months before Colette heard from her agent. In September she was back at school, her teaching kept her mind busy, and she enjoyed her work as an educator.

Her agent had found a publisher for her, who wanted to meet her and discuss future plans. The publisher, agent and Colette met during Saturday lunch. The publisher was enthusiastic about her book and CD idea. He expressed his disappointment that it was too late to be ready for the Christmas sale, as it would take a little longer to organize and publish the book and CD. He hoped to have it together before Easter.

He said: "I asked you here today to see if you would write another book, maybe it could be more Christmassy and have it ready for next year's Christmas."

Colette thought this over. She said: "Thanks for the offer, I would love to do this, but are you aware of the intricate process of three kinds of artists: the writing, painting and music all will have to come together, which will take some time and effort. I will have to discuss this with the artists. Mark Maxwell, the composer himself has a very busy life as Professor and musician."

The publisher and agent could understand this. The painter artist, Caroline Bromley, was a friend and she saw no difficulties there. Caroline, she was sure would have some lovely ideas for pictures.

The agent suggested another Saturday lunchtime meeting with the painter, writer and composer. This meeting was discussed during the week and Mark who was willing to cooperate, suggested that his brother James should come along as well to make sure that the contract was all right.

Mark, Colette, Caroline and James met with the publisher and agent. They all agreed to work together and have this Christmas book out before the end of November.

CHAPTER 10

Ashley's work with the band and the usual curriculum for teaching music kept her pretty occupied. There were band and choir competitions to be organized and different programs had to be set up for each level.

Among all these students she found this year two violinists at a Grade 8 conservatorium level. She suggested that they play certain pieces with the band. This was apparently sufficient encouragement for them to start studying in earnest. The parents mentioned that this had made a big difference for their offspring. The students themselves heard how much they had improved lately.

Ashley demonstrated her new bamboo flute and she helped the drums along giving a kind of Fijian rhythm, which these young people really loved to hear.

Besides her teaching she was on her last course for her doctorate, and she was finishing off her dissertation, which had to do with music therapy and appreciation for young children and teenagers.

At home she had to get used to making meals and cleaning the house. By the end of September Mark saw that it was too much for Ashley even though he helped out, but his time was also limited.

Colette's housekeeper Minah sent them her daughter, a young Philippina university student, who gladly helped out and even offered to get dinner ready on her days that she was working at Ashley's. This made a big improvement for them both. The young girl Asha was indeed a great help. Now their love for music and each other could come first.

Ashley found several piano students and had them play in her place while she was directing the junior band. Another young pianist played with the choir. The enjoyment that these young musicians got out of playing with the band or choir was unbelievable. Their parents saw the improvement and they told Ashley that they didn't need to prompt or nag their offspring to practice as they used to do.

Much later in the year she wondered if she could get a small group together for light classical music and maybe some country music. The two violinists plus Ashley on the violin and pianists were all for it. Three flautists, as well as a guitar, a drummer and a cymbal player joined the group.

The small orchestra had the desired effect as the boys and girls were encouraged by their success. Ashley showed them how the saxophone and other wind instruments gave liveliness to the music.

The principal was impressed and came up with the idea of a lunchtime concert for the school, but no compulsory attendance, so the non-music lovers could have their usual free time.

Teachers and principal were wondering how many students would turn up to listen to the classical concert. The small classical orchestra performed and at the end there was an outcry for an encore. Ashley asked the choir to sing their last learned song. They ended the concert with choir and band combined: "You'll Never Walk Alone."

After the performance the principal asked whether the audience would like to hear another concert later on in the year. There was 100% agreement. Ashley had tears in her eyes; she now knew that she was doing her job well. There was appreciation for good music.

Occasionally as for instance on Mark's birthday Ashley asked both their families for dinner. Asha, her helper came over and helped cook. Sometimes she would make her native dishes from the Philippines, which was greatly appreciated by the whole family. Sometimes they would make a gado-gado that is a sort of salad using all kinds of raw vegetables and hard boiled eggs with a spicy peanut-butter sauce.

Mark was asked to conduct a summer weekend tour through B.C. He started to organize the program and discussed this with Ashley and then came the rehearsing. The program had to be suitable for the summer evenings: light and happy music, maybe interlaced with some classical and country western music so that everyone could enjoy this concert, young and old.

Mark asked for the input of several members of the orchestra and also discussed the idea of directing while playing as he did not like to give up his violin playing. He just loved playing this instrument. To him it was the most beautiful sounding instrument. They tried this out a few times and all came to the conclusion that this was feasible and maybe a little different. Many other musicians played the piano and conducted. Ashley did this with her school band so why not while playing the violin.

Mark and his musicians worked hard at organizing a suitable program and Ashley helped along there too. She gave her input on the lighter fare. She was mostly in contact with young people and what attracted them. She understood their tastes.

These August concerts were especially put on to attract people of all ages and all walks of life. This program needed diversification.

Ashley could travel with Mark occasionally but she wanted to edit her dissertation one more time and send it in. She hoped it would be in good time for the October convocation.

All this was so demanding and it came so soon after their wedding. But they were young and energetic and Ashley could see that this was a good chance for Mark. It could be a start for his orchestra later on. She knew his thoughts were going in that direction; especially now that he was directing and playing his beloved instrument as well as directing.

The main orchestra was called the "Vancouver Symphony". Because the musicians in this ensemble were all a part of this Symphony, a new name was needed to attract the younger generation as well as the livelier seniors, who also enjoy toe-tapping rhythms.

Someone came up with the "Vancouver Festival Orchestra". The agent organized most of the concerts for the weekends and if it was possible and the weather was right they could play outside on a platform in the town square; but most concerts were in a hall or other suitable building.

Mark usually came home on Sunday night or early Monday morning.

The tour was short, but so successful that several cities asked for performances during the winter season. The agent thought this was feasible and would look into this. However most musicians had a regular job and played with the Symphony as well. But the Festival musicians were all young and enthusiastic about their tour. They thought they could have an occasional performance; possibly on Thanksgiving weekend in October. Kelowna was chosen for this concert. Maybe they could go to Victoria for a Christmas concert.

In September Mark began his teaching again at the University of B.C. and Ashley worked again with her High School music, teaching band, choir and theory. Her studies were finished and she was waiting for the outcome of her dissertation. Without her studies this year she could devote her spare time to being a loving wife to Mark and teaching her teenage students.

She was looking forward to a fairly normal year after the hectic time of studying and teaching as well as falling in love and getting married.

At the end of September she was notified that the committee had agreed to accept her dissertation and the date for convocation was set for the end of October.

Everyone in the family was so happy for her. She had achieved what she had set out to do. Mark took her out to dinner that night and gave her a large bouquet of red roses.

Again this year there would be a performance of a light operetta or a light musical at the school. All teachers, who were interested, put their heads together. It was such a big undertaking to organize this.

There were discussions on what to perform and why this was suitable for these youngsters. Ashley's colleagues suggested: *Mikado, Wizard of Oz* with that lovely song "Over the Rainbow", *Westside Story*, or Victor Herbert's *Babes in the Toyland* or would the *Sound of Music* be more suitable. Then it was mentioned that the lyrics of *H.M.S. Pinafore* would be lively and interesting to sing as "The Lass That Loved a Sailor," where the daughter of the Captain falls in love with a common sailor. This would be breezy and bright.

Then there was *Evita*.

The principal suggested giving the youngsters a choice just between the two musicals that were finally chosen by the Staff: either the *Mikado* or *H.M.S. Pinafore*.

Ashley played some of the lyrics of each musical. The final choice came to *H.M.S. Pinafore*. The boys especially liked that one.

Now the hard work could begin. At first with the staff only, discussing who was going to teach the words of the songs, the proper pronunciation and diction. Who would take care of the stage and costumes?

Ashley of course had all the music which meant: with the band and its different instruments, male choir, female choir and solos.

It all involved hard work, but it also was fun to hear these young people's comments and jokes and teasing. The best of it was that they all loved working on this project. They gave up many lunch times for rehearsals as did many of the teachers. They had started in rehearsals in early October, which would give them plenty of time, so that the academic work did not need to suffer. On the contrary there was an uplifting attitude and an atmosphere of high spirits in the school. The students were more involved. There were not many bored faces.

Then it was time for Ashley's convocation. Nothing much was said about this. Mom and Dad and Mark were attending. That was all. Mark as professor was sitting on the podium with all the other profs dressed in their colorful regalia. But what Ashley did not know was that Mark was to hand his wife the Ph.D. certificate. He had not been her prof. these last two years, but the committee thought it fitting to have Mark hand his wife the diploma. She was so surprised and then when he kissed her as well on the podium, the audience applauded and cheered.

Mark's father took both families out to dinner. Afterwards they were going to Mark and Ashley's home for coffee and dessert. Colette said she had made a cake for the occasion. Mark's brothers were at the house already.

What a surprise Ashley got when she with Mark by her side, entered the spacious living room. She noticed it immediately; she paled and looked around at the family right behind her. In her wildest dreams she had never thought of owning this beautiful instrument. She just stood there shocked. Mark took her in his arms saying: "Congratulations, you deserve this for all your hard work. This is a present from both families. They all love you so much."

He took her over to the grand piano and sat her down. She tried a few bars, she was absolutely enraptured. The tone was so beautiful, pure and deep. Then she went to thank everyone. She didn't know what to say; she was stunned! Ashley was not the only emotional person in this room! Colette kissed Ashley with tears in her eyes. She and Andrew were so happy for their daughter and so proud of her achievements.

How had they organized this surprise? She had never noticed anything brewing.

Ashley went again to the beautiful Steinway and touched it; still not believing her eyes. Mark's brothers had been involved in getting the piano inside and installed exactly where Mark had indicated. Then there was indeed the coffee, liquor and dessert to top off the evening.

On the last period on Fridays the students at this school were allowed to choose their own favorite subject. It could be music, poetry, art, chess, woodwork or history. There were no exams required for this work.

This time however the principal announced that all students and staff were required in the Auditorium. In all innocence Ashley went there with her class, but then she was escorted to the stage where the principal and school board president congratulated her. He pointed out to the audience that: "Mrs. Maxwell now, Dr. Maxwell, had set an example to all students. She has obtained a Ph. D. in Music and now she is Dr. Maxwell. This shows what ambition and hard work can accomplish. We won't be surprised if some of you will manage something like this."

He signaled to a boy and a girl who presented her with a huge bouquet from staff and students.

Ashley felt like walking on clouds. She was all done in. Her students were always joking around, they said: "Do we call you Dr. Maxwell now?"

She answered: "No like you were doing up to now, call me Mrs. Maxwell".

The couple had discussed whether Ashley should keep her maiden name or not. Ashley decided to take her husband's name. She would be a Maxwell.

Ashley realized that Mark was very satisfied with her decision. Ashley also noticed that Mark was more open with her and not as he used to be, non-communicative, like at the time when it nearly broke up their relationship.

At home Mark teased her now and then and called her Dr. Maxwell and she would say: "Which one are you calling?"

They had Mark's study insulated so that he could play there anytime without disturbing anyone and he would not be hindered by outside noises. Ashley could play her new grand anytime and not feel guilty making different sounds. She was now practicing the *H.M.S. Pinafore.* She had to know this music by heart in order to direct and play at the same time. So study she did. But it was not a punishment for her to play her lovely new instrument.

Now and then Mark would sneak in and accompany her on his violin. They liked playing together in more ways than this one.

They were able to discuss the music, where Mark suggested for instance a different way of expressing certain phrases.

They also worked and edited Colette's children's book. Mark had composed the music for some of the verses and they played these together.

The publisher had a CD company manufacture the CD and finally at the end of November the book and the enclosed CD were ready for sale at the stores for Christmas.

The Press critics thought it to be one of the best children's books on the market and it was advertised as an excellent Christmas present. And indeed it was a best seller in this genre.

Everyone was so happy for Colette. She needed this spiritual uplift after her son's accident and death. Andrew too was so proud of her.

They knew that the book was a success but they were shocked and surprised when Colette was called by her publisher weeks later, who asked her to come and receive the Children's Literature award. Mark and Caroline too, were included in the acknowledgements for the music and art contribution. What accomplishments and success in one gifted artistic family. But also what an amount of hard work, energy and talent were involved here!

Newspapers sent their journalists for interviews which also encouraged the sale of this book.

Their busy life continued. They kept up their Saturday dinners with the Maxwell family and the young couple was generally at Colette and Andrew's place on Sundays. Occasionally Mark and Ashley entertained both families at their house.

With all their work and responsibilities Ashley and Mark were looking forward to Easter. They did not plan anything special for these holidays. They were just going to relax and play music if they felt like it. Their whole world so far was making beautiful music.

It was nearing the end of the year and it was time for *H.M.S. Pinafore* to be presented. They were going to perform this musical three nights in a row. In preparation for this they had an afternoon rehearsal for the school. On the last evening of the production the Superintendant from Vancouver Joe Stern had invited his friend and colleague from Bellingham, Washington to attend. Dan Cooper was so impressed with the performance that he asked Joe if it would be at all possible for Ashley to bring the performance to Bellingham.

Joe Stern discussed this with the principal and the school board members. After some deliberation it was agreed to go to Bellingham. The school board arranged the bus transport. There was some more rehearsing and then the group left for Bellingham in high spirits. They were received by the superintendent, school board members and the students of that high school in Bellingham. Mr. Cooper had been able to get the city's auditorium for this performance. Music lovers attended this presentation. Many in the audience had attended concerts in Vancouver and surroundings and were impressed by the performance. The Bellingham superintendant introduced himself to Ashley who told her that he had enjoyed not only the musical but had noticed her manner of directing it and conducting the band. He said; "That was really professional work. You should think about conducting an orchestra professionally." Ashley answered him; "Thank you those are very kind words. My students worked very hard and enjoyed working on this performance. And indeed I have thought of directing my own orchestra. I even took courses on conducting when I was in Europe."

Mr. Cooper had brought a friend along from Seattle, Richard Nottingdale, who was on the Symphony board there. He too was impressed by the result of Ashley's work. He actually was excited about the way Ashley conducted and got such good response from her student orchestra which he thought was due to her way of conducting. Little did Ashley know that upon Nottingdale's return to Seattle he reported to the board of directors about what he had seen and heard in Bellingham.

Ashley was surprised to receive a letter asking her to come for an audition in Seattle to conduct the Symphony there! She showed the letter to Mark, who in turn showed this letter to the Vancouver Symphony board. Since Ashley lived in Vancouver she wanted to stay there as her husband was established as Symphony conductor and university prof. Ashley answered that she had to decline but thanked them for their offer.

Lately they had been thinking of starting a family before they became too old to enjoy busy little children. Ashley's career would have to suffer; because she would want to stay at home and see their children grow up from babyhood at least until kindergarten. She became pregnant and everything seemed fine until the fourth month when she lost the baby. Tests showed she had a shortage of folic acid and she was somewhat overworked. The doctor advised her to take it easy for a while and try for another baby later on. She needed a good rest first.

Of course they were pretty sad and disappointed, but the doctor assured them that there was no reason why she could not have a healthy baby after taking medicine, a good rest and a holiday.

Mark's dreams of playing with his daughter or son were shattered for the time being, as well as his dreams of playing music to their off-spring. Both Ashley and he had been wondering whether their children would be gifted in music or other arts. With parents as musicians, grandmother as writer and great-grandfather was a painter; their children might be artistic too.

Ashley's and Mark's parents were disappointed and sad for their sake, but nothing could be done about this. Life has to go on!

That summer Mark took extra good care of Ashley. He made sure that she rested every afternoon or when they came home from an outing. Mark had joined again the Vancouver Festival orchestra and Ashley traveled with him if the trip was not too tiresome. She also substituted now and then as pianist or violinist if one of the members could not make it, which worked out very well for everyone. Ashley loved to play anyway and now with her darling husband conducting this was a double enjoyment.

They were not the only husband and wife team in the music world. They had friends in Toronto where the wife was a harpist and the husband was the conductor.

They visited beautiful areas or interesting buildings in the different cities and towns in which they gave concerts.

Their agent had organized weekend tours to Seattle, Vancouver, Washington, Victoria, Nanaimo and Kelowna, ending in Penticton at the end of August.

This working-holiday had done them a lot of good. They were rested and ready to tackle a new school year. Everything should be a little easier for Ashley this year. She knew what to expect, or did she?

Surprises were daily possibilities which were exactly the reason why teaching was never boring, it was rather the contrary.

Ashley had often heard her mother say: "I wonder what some of my pupils will do today?"

One day after Christmas Mark came home and mentioned that Ashley's dissertation had been discussed. The profs on the advisory committee were saying that it was a pity that there was no continuation of this therapy and more research was needed. "What could be done about this? Actually the author of this dissertation should continue the work in this field."

Mark spoke up, he said: "You know that this is my wife, her name was Van Heekeren when she wrote this."

This was a surprise! The members of this committee wondered if she could come aboard. That meant, could she come and work as music prof at the University. She had all the qualifications and more to teach at University level. But first they had to propose this to the board and see what would happen there.

Mark of course spilled the beans and told Ashley all about the ideas that had been thrown about and that her name had come up.

"What do you think about this idea, Dr. Maxwell?" he asked teasingly.

"I must say, this is my pet project and it needs a lot more research as well as trying out many groups and at different levels. But if I would join this group I would not be able to have my band and choir."

Mark thought this over and said: "Eventually you could do this same work with the University music students, that is, if there is an opening."

As this did not seem to be the case they continued their music making and teaching until in February Mark told her that the music therapy had come up again and they wanted to know if Ashley would be interested in continuing this project and fill in for the Music Education Professor, who was retiring at the end of the year. This would mean instructing teachers' in Music Education with band and choir at University level. Did Ashley have ears for this!!

They discussed this thoroughly and also with her parents. Colette and Andrew agreed that this would be just right for Ashley as she was so involved in this therapy project. Ashley as well as Colette were convinced that with the help of a certain kind of music some or maybe many children and adults could be helped. Ashley and other musicians knew that music brought peace, satisfaction and relaxation to numerous people, which is so necessary in our competitive noisy world.

Ashley applied officially and she was accepted as prof at the Education Department with four days a week teaching music to the student-teachers and for the time being one day a week for Music Therapy Research. She could combine her research with her teaching, and via these Education students she would be in contact with children and teenagers when she had to go to the schools to observe her students in practice-teaching.

Most of the time Mark and his precious wife could travel together to and from the U, unless there were meetings for either Mark or Ashley.

Ashley notified the school board in good time giving them plenty of opportunity to find another music teacher.

She had several meetings with the retiring prof. who prepared her for her new job. During her holidays in July and August she worked on lesson-plans and started her research on Music Therapy.

With more music education in schools this could bring help to many from a young age on, when not only children are more perceptive but help can be given at the start of trouble, before it is too late.

There are different treatments which could be combined

with the music therapy and therefore might be more effective.

Ashley was going to have a look at other therapies and disorder treatments and get in contact with several psychologists at the University.

But actually she was more interested in bringing more music into the schools and with that the academic subjects would not suffer, on the contrary it had been proven that it can be very beneficial. As for instance last year's High School performance where the students had more energy and they were not as the youngsters call it "bored". The result was that music and other arts as well as the academics had improved.

Ashley found that athletics played a superior role in the school systems. She had to agree that sports are beneficial. Indeed, everyone should be given a chance to experience different sports but not everyone is keen on sports.

Time needs to be divided between sports and the arts. After all sports can be enjoyed for such a short time in a person's life, while music, or any other art is a pleasure for the rest of one's life. Even the very old, can play an instrument or at least listen to and appreciate beautiful or lively music for the rest of their lives.

In all there had been a positive effect on behavior as well as on the results of the academic subjects.

Besides singing, listening and playing instruments there does not seem to be any time for students to compose their own music. Few youngsters are ever encouraged to do this. For instance writing short poems or even a haiku and then sing their own tune to this is an amusing exercise for children. Here again encouragement with sensitivity and caring, stimulates success. Composing is a spontaneous expression.

Time is the problem. According to Ashley half an hour could be added to the school time, which is done with sports on a regular basis. This should be manageable.

Ashley taught her music students that attitude, posture

and facial expression were important to convey the message of the song and music, which is actually interpreting the melody. She used to say:"Would you like to look at an orchestra with sour unhappy looking players? Smile or show a happy face or even a sad face when the music is sad, or show emotions when you are done in by the sound of the music you are playing as with the "Sonata Pathetic" by Beethoven or "Sibelius Finlandia." Ashley showed that Sibelius is longing for his home, Finland

Youngsters are especially attracted to rhythm and that at a very young age. They react by clapping their little hands or jumping and dancing with the music long before they can speak.

Most youngsters improve their behavioral problems and control their impulsivity because they learn a certain discipline in playing or singing. That discipline may turn into love for music.

Ashley discussed this with her husband saying: "I am not so much interested in clinical therapy. My main interest is more the general benefit of music for students at all school levels, making it a healing project, by making music that is instilling hope and beauty for life."

She went on: "There is music within each person. Every musical experience could be a life experience. It may encourage self-expression and spontaneity. Music is an art beyond measure."

All this she often discussed with Mark, who gave her his input or sometimes other ideas. They both thought that Ashley was going to have an exciting year. This excitement must have been too much for this newly married couple. Upon returning from giving a concert in Victoria, where they had also gone for a long walk before boarding the ferry, they missed the ferry and then came home very late, totally exhausted.

Ashley lost her temper and Mark did not react too well to that. He shouted back at her and hid himself in his room.

Of course he played his violin, drowning his sadness about this silly quarrel. After about an hour of intensive playing he had calmed down and his music became softer and more subdued.

When he had calmed down, he went to see his wife. He found her fast asleep under an afghan on the couch. He could see she had cried herself to sleep. He picked her up and carried her to bed. When she did not wake up he realized that she was overtired.

He joined her soon and kept on thinking about what had happened? They had never shouted at each other. This was such a shock to him. He knew it happened in most marriages, but he just had not expected this to happen to him and Ashley. He was bowled over by both their reactions. He made a vow that this would not happen again if he could help it. He planned to discuss this with Ashley.

When Ashley woke up next morning she felt ashamed and did not know what to do. But Mark took her in his arms. They hugged and promised that they would be more careful with each other. They knew they had hurt each other so thoroughly and swore to try and avoid these situations. They were sure it would happen again, as with most people, but they promised each other to try to reason out the situation rather than fly into anger. But they would try their best. Mark planned to see that they would not get as overtired as they were last night.

University life started soon for both of them. Mark was involved with the Vancouver Philharmonic Orchestra as well, and being the concert-master there were many things to organize, besides studying and performing. Often when he played at home Ashley would accompany him either on the piano or the violin. This was their relaxation as well. At the U. he had his regular music classes of students working toward their degree in music.

Ashley taught music in general for the student-teachers

with the aspect of how to bring music and love for music to the children in their classrooms.

Ashley told her classes that she wanted to start an orchestra. Anyone who wanted to join should sign the list with their telephone number and instrument they played and how many years of experience they had. Beginners were to sign the other sheet.

In her classes she explained that beginners were very welcome. During lunchtime she helped the want-to-be musicians get a chance to learn a favorite instrument and join a group of young musicians.

Of course there had to be a University choir. Ashley had such fun organizing all these activities and classes. There were more beginners than she had expected, but several would quit before long. Working with the advanced musicians was lots of fun. She had to work mostly on bringing the intensity of sound down.

So many young adults were used to bar and nightclub blaring. She had to inform them that not only their ears would suffer from this sound-attack, but loudness or noise as she called this, did not bring any beauty or happiness to the music. She told them to listen to their own playing and put their soul in the playing. "Let yourself feel the music."

In her regular student-teacher classes she brought out the importance of music therapy and how these future teachers could use this in their classes.

When she was supervising the students, she made copious notes on the pupil's behavior in music classes.

In the classroom she could show what she meant when she had told her students to observe and notice the behavior and interest of the children.

She also showed in the classroom just how a little encouragement and praise could work and not only with music.

Because this improved self-confidence was brought over to the whole child.

For Christmas she had organized the choir and orchestra. They performed at lunchtimes at different areas of the campus.

Mark came to at least one of the performances and of course he was very pleased with the result of Ashley's work.

Ashley accompanied Mark at night when he had rehearsals with the Philharmonic so that she could keep up to date with their music in case she was called upon to substitute either for piano or violin. Of course the whole family attended the concert performed just before Christmas. It was a wonderful program. This time all musicians were present. Ashley could enjoy the concert with her parents and in-laws. After the performance they all went for a drink and enjoyed each other's company.

Mark's brothers were there with their wives. The brothers were as usual teasing and joking. The Maxwell seniors were happy to see all their children content again. They had all suffered during James's scandal. Now that this trouble was dissolved, everyone was on top of the world.

Ashley's family too needed a happy atmosphere after the loss of their son.

Mark and Ashley took it easy during the Christmas holidays. They just looked at their plans for the New Year and made up some programs. And they played their music, alone or together, always trying to perfect their expression of their playing.

They stayed a few days just north of Sechelt and visited the ribbon like waterfalls and listened to the singing waters as they came down and they dreamt.

As the poet Tennyson said: "We live in our dreams."

They just sat and admired the view and obtained inspiration.

CHAPTER 11

Rested and relaxed they started the new school year, working and making music.

They were going to try and have another baby. But, so far no luck! They did not worry much about it; they were so busy anyway.

The regular conductor of the Philharmonic became very ill and Mark stepped in his place for the time being, but he suggested that he play his violin while conducting. He just could not see not playing his violin. To him it was his lifeline. In his deep expression of music he needed the feel, the rhythm and meaning of his instrument. With his violin he expressed vigor, nuances, smooth flow indicating the poetry and elegance of music.

He felt he could take the orchestra along showing passionate emotions as well as happy, boisterous feelings, full of vitality.

The orchestra being all professionals and the best musicians, agreed. Mark needed another concert-master, whom he found in Jim Walker, his best friend and friend of the Maxwell family.

Ashley was asked to fill in for Jim, but she thought she had too much on her plate already. She promised to study the programs in case someone could not attend, and then she would substitute.

The school year flew by. Before they knew it there was May and the final exams. Then June came with its convocations and graduations. This was always such a busy time with many meetings to attend and even plans to make for next September.

Mark was asked to teach a course at the Sorbonne in July and two weeks in August and Ashley had heard that the University in Paris had courses on Music Therapy. She thought she might learn new ideas that would help her in her research. She also took another course in conducting an orchestra.

They both flew to Paris, where they stayed for six weeks in a lovely apartment. In their spare time Mark took Ashley to see interesting buildings and they attended Mass at old remarkable churches. They visited Chartres and Tours on weekends and attended Mass at the beautiful Cathedral in Reims They loved the landscape south of Paris, Reims. They found the country side there so fantastic. It was full summer, with the golden-yellow ripening wheat set against the dark green cypress trees.

They came home satisfied and happy to see their parents again. All their adventures and experiences had to be told.

Ashley mentioned to Colette the new ideas she had learned and what she could use in her book later about music therapy. Her ideas about writing that book grew by the day as well as the notes she had collected on this subject. But she needed still more research, which she hoped to get during the school year when her student-teachers were practicing her views and theories to youngsters aged six to eighteen.

She wanted to prove that the result of this therapy would flow over into interest of other subjects and actually a better attitude towards life.

They still were not too worried about not getting any babies. Ashley would have liked a little boy with his father's love for music. She could just imagine a little Mark with his violin or a little girl with her Dad's dark curls, following her beloved Dad.

They did everything the doctor had told them to do, which was mainly don't worry. But towards the end of the school year they went to see a specialist. They told him about the miscarriage. He examined Ashley and took all sorts of tests. The outcome was perfect and there was no reason for not having a baby. He said: "Just enjoy your life and give it two years. Then we will see again."

They returned home and enjoyed each other. They certainly had no problem in that area.

Ashley took a lighter load of teaching. Now she had two days for organizing her notes and writing the book on therapy.

As the concert hall was not always filled Mark wondered if there would be room in Vancouver's society for a lighter more upbeat, buoyant orchestra, giving an opportunity for public involvement.

Maybe a small choir accompanying the orchestra now and then, singing joyful, jubilant songs by a vivacious young group would be attractive to the audience. As Mark said, "Classical music does not need to be pompous or serious, but it does not appeal to everyone, why don't we try to attract these people?"

Several months later the music agent came up with an idea to have a concert during the Christmas holidays, maybe one performance in Vancouver and one in Victoria.

The whole orchestra agreed and as this occurred during the holidays Ashley would join as violinist. The right music for Christmas was organized and rehearsed. All the musicians were wondering how this would work out. They were all a bit leery. This kind of music had not been performed in Vancouver and certainly not in staid Victoria.

Here came the "Vancouver Festival Orchestra", and unbelievably they took the concert goers by storm.

After the first opening piece they knew they had a winner. The applause was overwhelming. The musicians became even more enthusiastic if that was possible. They all glowed with pleasure while playing and this time they included the public with their clapping on the rhythm of a lively march called "March of the Toy Soldiers" by Tchaikovsky.

Then they followed with a love song and a romantic classic which was received with the same enthusiasm and on again to a waltz then a sing-along happy song and "Going My Way" which used to be sung by Frank Sinatra.

Ashley was surprised to see how well Mark interacted with the concert-goers. He was funny as he got the people involved. But then she thought yes that's how he is with his students; light-hearted and happy, instilling love for music in every variety.

Both concerts were an enormous success. They had a standing ovation and many bravos, which deserved an encore in the form of a hand clapping march.

The Maxwells as well as Ashley's parents had attended these concerts. They had been in for a formidable surprise. They really had no idea that their son could perform so happily and more or less act as a clown before the public. His brothers had always overshadowed him in the teasing and joking department.

Indeed this was what Vancouver needed. The Maxwell brothers thought it was hilarious to see their "little quiet" brother performing and being so funny. They did not know that he had that funny streak in him. The whole family met afterwards in the hotel for a drink.

Ashley and Mark thought up another idea; what about performing this kind of concert for the schools. Many children would not get a chance to hear first class musicians. This would open up a whole new world for them. He could show the different instruments and their sounds as well as various kinds of music. Not too many children have been to a concert, they may enjoy seeing and hearing an orchestra. Economics would play a large role in this effort. Also seeing and hearing an orchestra might open up an interest in music and its instruments.

Mark and Ashley discussed this and Mark brought the idea to the committee of the Vancouver Festival Orchestra and school board members. Quite a few members of the orchestra agreed that something could be done in that direction. They promised their help and suggested all kinds of light happy music, suitable for children; interspersed by romantic melodies and love songs. But also semi-classical music with a cadence should be played.

They no sooner thought about it and all the wheels were put into motion. At first it was said it would be too expensive to move so many children around, rent a theatre, have so many buses driving and above all miss that much school time. The committee found two large schools with auditoriums and cooperative principals, one was in the inner city school, one was in the suburbs. They could manage the two schools in one afternoon.

Where there is a will there is a way. A school bus would transport the orchestra. A small committee was organized to arrange a suitable concert program for teenagers and one fitting for younger children. They had found some surprising pieces; they put in some comedy making the youngsters laugh. Songs like: "Send in the Clowns", "Happy Days are Here Again", "The Entertainer," marches, but also romantic love songs, dreamy emotional music and of course this was interspersed by classical music. "The Syncopated Clock" was appreciated, as well as a part of "Beethoven's ninth symphony", and back again to a happy march. Mark planned to involve the youngsters by letting them clap in time of the beat. They especially liked the "March of the Toy Soldiers" in the Nutcracker Suite.

Just before the Easter break seemed an excellent timing.

The applause afterward was terrific. It was a great success and hopefully the students had experienced a musical enrichment.

With all their busy life of organizing this concert and their regular work they had been too busy to think of getting a baby. It certainly came as a surprise to them when they found that Ashley was pregnant. They were so ecstatic about it. Mark was clowning around and of course told his parents and Ashley's mother and father. Although they need not tell Colette, she could read from their faces that something extra-ordinary was happening to them.

They all celebrated and started to make plans. Mark would like her to stay at home. At first Ashley was not too happy about that; she was feeling so well. But as Mark pointed out: "Working with student-teachers is a lot of work and traveling to the different schools to see them teach is very tiring. Why don't you stay home and finish your book and then you could play more with the orchestra, which you seem to enjoy so much."

She agreed, so she resigned from her position at the University. They were going to take the summer off and travel to the east coast, visiting friends and family along the way.

Around the time they arrived in Montreal Ashley found that she needed some information for her book. Both of them went to the music department at the University there and not only found the input she needed but they discovered a former student working in the music department as assistant-prof. He was so helpful in finding the right people to meet. And indeed Ashley received quite an amount of information.

Mark was introduced to a Music Prof. who also was a musician in the Montreal Philharmonic. They knew of each other, but had never met. The two men agreed to have dinner together and bring their wives. During the conversation Mark brought up the subject of the "Vancouver Festival Orchestra", which Mark had conducted in Vancouver. This Prof. Maurice

St. Denis was a cellist and his wife Lucille was a harpist. They were both very interested in the kind of program Mark and his orchestra had developed.

They got along so well together that they planned to meet for breakfast before Mark and Ashley left for Nova Scotia.

When they met the next morning, Mark, being so sensitive to other people‘s moods, could see that something was bothering Maurice. After they had ordered, Mark asked if something was worrying him. Maurice said: "You certainly bring me straight to the subject of my worries. When we came home last night, there was a telephone message from the wife of the conductor. Her husband had broken a hip and now what were they to do about the concert in three weeks time?"

Maurice said: "I got in contact with some of the orchestra and the management. As these are holidays we are now in a bind. I have been so bold as to suggest you, Mark as guest-conductor. What about it?"

Ashley, looking at Mark, thought to herself I can see he would like to do this. She nodded at him "if you want to do it, why not".

Mark then said: "I am interested, I have my violin with me as always; can you get the music for the program, so that I can study this during my trip to Nova Scotia?"

Maurice finished his meal and went to the telephone. Half an hour later he came back beaming, all his worries gone. He had spoken to the agent and the concert-master. So far everything was okay. The agent and concert-master were coming over to Maurice's house with the music if that was alright with Mark and Ashley. They could discuss contract and rehearsals there.

What a day this was! They followed Lucille and Maurice to their lovely home SE of Montreal. After the meeting with the agent and concert-master, they could be on their way east to Halifax. Ashley and Mark would return three or four days before the concert for rehearsals. Maurice and Mark discussed the program and the music. Mark also mentioned directing while playing and they agreed they would work this out during the rehearsals.

Mark and Ashley went on their trip enjoying the scenery on the way. They drove around the coast of Nova Scotia and Cape Breton Island taking pleasure in the wild waters splashing against the rocks, taking in the atmosphere and beauty of the landscapes, giving them plenty of inspiration.

At night in their hotel room they studied and played. They were so happy and upbeat. These two people certainly shared beautiful sounds and thoughts. They always tried to get a room where others would not be bothered by their music.

Ashley was now about three months pregnant and she was feeling so well, she could not believe herself that she was carrying a living doll.

They stayed a few days in Halifax visiting the harbor and old buildings.

They returned to Montreal and phoned their new friends Maurice and Lucille, who immediately asked them over for supper. They could then discuss times for rehearsals.

The rehearsals were very intense and tiring. Ashley sometimes came along to listen.

Mark showed how he directed while playing his violin. Being professional, energetic musicians they were all for trying out Mark's method. They were astonished how well this worked and if this was what Mark liked then they would fit in.

The concert was a great success. The public appreciated that Mark was substituting at such short notice. They had enjoyed the music and the manner in which it was played. The applause was tremendous. They wanted more - more.

Mark and the orchestra gave an encore, but of a lighter genre and this was equally well received. Of course Ashley enjoyed her husband's playing and conducting as usual.

After visiting the important buildings and churches in

Montreal they traveled home at a leisurely pace enjoying the surroundings along the way.

It was getting toward the end of summer with the environment still so beautiful and the flowers were at their best.

Sometimes they would stay overnight to look around and have a restful day or make a short trip if there was something remarkable to be seen. A leisurely tour through British Columbia's mountains gave Mark inspiration. If he heard the melody in his head, while driving, they stopped early that day. He needed to play back that tune and compose the notes.

This trip seemed to have been good for both of them. They came home ready to tackle their jobs. For Ashley this would be a little different as she was not going to teach this year. She was putting all her attention and energy on her music therapy book. She had done most of the research. She could write at home and occasionally go to the U. to get more information.

Upon returning from their trip Ashley went to see her doctor. He advised her to see a specialist because of her history. She was doing fine so far, but he wanted to be extra sure. He organized the visit to the specialist in two weeks time.

That doctor wanted her to get an ultra sound. He said there was nothing to worry about: "We do this regularly". Mark came along because he wanted to see their child. That happened to be a good idea because there was a great surprise for both of them. There was not just one tiny baby, but two were moving around. They just could not believe it. The doctor was not sure about the sex of the babies. In another month they would look at another ultra sound. For now everything was normal and the babies looked sound and healthy.

Mark and Ashley were quite shocked. Mark said: "We don't do things in halves, do we?" Once they had recovered they were excited. They would have a real family. They knew too that these two babies would give them an enormous amount of work, but they would manage.

That weekend they told their parents about their little

surprises. The parents were so happy for them. They were all starting to think of names for both sexes. They made up lists. Ashley wanted a little Mark, but two Marks in the family could be very confusing. Then they thought Tom and Mark as a middle name. Or Ted and Sean or Alison and Patrick, then someone suggested Ainsley and Raoul.

Mark and Ashley were glad they did not have to decide yet for five months. All they had to do now was dream up some suitable names and they were both good at dreaming.

Colette too dreamt; she dreamt up a story or poem for her new grandchildren and she would ask Mark to have a look at the book and see if he could set the words to music. She was going to make it in poem form, suitable for very young children.

Everyone was making plans. Marks parents had stored the baby furniture which had also been used for Sean's and Alysson's children.

The house needed to be reorganized with a small room downstairs for the babies, so that Ashley would not have to run upstairs during the day every time one or both of them cried.

Ashley worked hard to get the book finished before the little ones were born. She missed the teaching and the musical performances, the interrelation with students and staff. Her name stayed however as substitute pianist and violinist with the Philharmonic. She generally went with Mark to his rehearsals. That way she kept her playing up to date and also she was with Mark as well.

They were looking forward to the next ultra sound, when, they would find out the sex of their children. The future parents were reading and learning as much as they could about babies, but especially twin babies.

The ultra sound was again quite amazing. The two babies were boys! The doctor said: "Well, you are going to be parents of twin boys and they could be identical".

My goodness, twin boys! Surprises galore in this family!

Sean, Mark's teasing brother joked: "How are we going to ban two violins out of the bathroom?" Mark piped up: "What about three violins, I'm the oldest, so I am first!"

They could see a lot of little problems arising, especially if they were identical twins.

Now one big question was what are the names going to be? Girls' names could be written off now. Everyone came up with boys names. There were Tom and Tim, Gary, Gordon or Glenn, James and Sean, but these last ones might become too confusing. Then there were Robert (Bob) and Raymond or Richard (Rick).

Colette suggested: "Let's wait and see how they look. If they are totally different you may change your ideas. They may act so dissimilar, and they are going to be their own personality and we may all have trouble setting them apart. This is for sure going to be fun. Thinking about all this is going to make me want to write a book about twin boys. I am having fun already thinking up a story with twin boys in it."

Others certainly may have difficulty keeping them apart. More names came up: Tom and Robbie, Aidan and Tom, Andrew and Sean. And THE day was coming nearer all the time.

In the meantime Andrew and Colette had been dreaming up a surprise. Their house had been too large for just the two of them since Tom died and Ashley got married. And now with two little boys coming they wanted to be closer to Ashley and her family and they looked forward to less housework. Andrew and Colette had found an apartment with a lovely view over the ocean, two bedrooms and a closed-in insulated balcony, which could be used for a den or office for both of them. This sunroom had such a wonderful view overlooking gardens down below and further away they could see the surf and shipping going past. The apartment was closer to Andrew's office, which shortened his travelling time. This area was fairly close to Mark and Ashley and was so lovely, with towering old trees and large well-kept homes with lovely gardens around.

Colette dropped another bombshell. She wanted to retire and spend more time on her writing and of course she was thinking of helping Ashley with the babies and babysitting the twins. Also the publishers had been enamored with the books and pictures drawn by the friend/artist. They were asking for more books.

Andrew had always wanted to live on Sechelt, but he knew that as long as he was working that traveling to and fro would be out of the question. The ferry was not such a long trip, but the waiting to get on board could be rather lengthy especially during the summer. Now they could start looking around for their dream view and house, they would not rush into anything.

Andrew and Colette had spent most of their holidays in Gibson or Sechelt. Sometimes they went sailing and what better territory is there than Howe Sound or the Strait of Georgia, sailing to Pender harbor or up to Powel River was so relaxing for them. Looking up to Mount Elphinstone is awesome. Later, when Andrew would retire they wanted to build or buy a small house on the Sunshine coast with a view. There were some beautiful spots there. The main question was getting an affordable and suitable lot. They kept their eyes open for a small house, but now that they had the apartment, they were not in a hurry.

Mark and Ashley celebrated Mark's homecoming after his concerts. He was always so happy to be home again and see his lovely wife.

Mark had to tell her all about the concert and the results. How he had enjoyed playing and how enthusiastic the musicians were. He told her about the applause and bravos from the public. She remembered how he had the whole class at the University in stitches and then again let them listen to solemn, emotional melodies or a heart rendering composition. Ashley could imagine how Mark communicated with the instrumentalists as well as the concert goers. She remembered how he acted in his music classes. He was known for his humor as well as showing the different emotions expressed by the various kinds of music or instruments. Then again he would discuss and play happy toe-tapping music.

She could visualize his actions while directing the orchestra. He demanded attention, which was fully given.

Occasionally he came home with a bouquet that the audience had presented, but most often he gave these flowers to one of the female musicians.

Ashley had managed all right in Mark's absence. She had established a workable routine in general with the aid of her helper.

Colette had an idea brewing in her mind of writing a novel, but she needed more time for that. Andrew liked his work and did not want to retire yet, but Colette thought she might see more of the babies and eventually help Ashley with the little boys.

The next few months they were all kept busy with their regular work, moving Colette and Andrew to the apartment, as well as organizing the nursery, a small room downstairs for babies' sleeping during the day and sleeping at night upstairs, to minimize Ashley's running up and down the stairs.

The families Van Heekeren and Maxwells were still mulling over names for the boys. What a puzzle! As if choosing one name was not enough! They had to think that those little babies had to live with their names for the rest of their lives.

The time of their birth came nearer and still no decision had been made. Someone thinking of this musical family came up with Joseph and Johan, or Jo and John? But Ashley could not see these two little ones waltzing through life.

One rehearsal night Ashley was feeling rather tired. She

planned to stay home and go to bed early. Mark made sure his wife was okay. She still had more than a month of waiting for her babies, so they were not imminent yet. Off he went.

Instead of rest doing her good, Ashley felt more miserable by the minute. Then pains came and went. She phoned her Mom, who was there in five minutes with Andrew. Colette saw that her daughter was in so much pain. They phoned the doctor, who said to come to the hospital immediately; he would be there. The hospital had been warned and the gurney was waiting to roll her inside, where the doctor was ready to examine her. He looked worried. He was not her specialist. Ashley was not due to have her baby for another month and the pain was constant now, but she was not opening up.

In the meantime Andrew had phoned Mark at his rehearsal and left a message to come to the hospital immediately. Half an hour later Mark arrived at his wife's bedside. It was hard seeing his darling wife suffering so much, and he could not do anything, until it hit him: phone his mother *Mrs. Baby Doctor*. He told her: "Mother, she is in so much pain and there is no space between the pains."

"I'll be over in five minutes", she said.

Mark told Ashley that his mother was coming which seemed to quiet her down a little. She appeared to have confidence in her mother-in-law.

And indeed the moment Mrs. Maxwell Sr. arrived; she reviewed the case with the doctor, then listened to the hearts of her grandsons and sternly told them: "Quick a cesarean or you'll have three deaths".

Mark was hustled out and Ashley was brought to the surgery, where she was delivered of the two boys just in the nick of time.

Everything had happened so fast since Dr. Maxwell Sr. had arrived, but to poor Mark it seemed more like a year. He kept on seeing Ashley's face so gray and worn out. She had looked hopeless and frightened. He made himself a promise that although he loved children he was not going to have Ashley go through this suffering again. He'd have a vasectomy or something.

Finally his mother came to tell him and Ashley's parents that everything was okay now. She saw Mark's face, all drawn and worried. She knew how much he had suffered and how upset he still was.

Ashley was still unconscious but she would soon be all right. The boys were on oxygen, but they were doing fine. Mark, Colette and Andrew could come along and see the little scraps. Mark was surprised how good they looked. He had expected them to be scrawny little things because they had entered the world a little too early. But they were five pounds each, which was not bad for twins. *Mrs. Baby Dr.* told them that they would be breathing on their own in one or two days.

Mark was in awe seeing these two little babies,' his and Ashley's sons. Then he thought again about Ashley and how much she had had to suffer and how close he had been to losing her. He wanted to see her, but he was told to wait until she was awake.

He just stood there looking at his sons, realizing what a responsibility he now had to bring them up and help them to become decent and giving human beings. They were now fast asleep. Mark thought: They are probably tuckered out from all the work they had done and they surely had been in a hurry to come into the world.

He could not see the color of their eyes, but they could change later anyway. Their hair seemed dark and curly; a true Maxwell feature.

The nurse called Mark to come and see his wife. When Mark saw Ashley he ran to her saying: "Oh, my dear, I thought I was losing you, I could not live without you. You must know that. I don't tell you often enough that I love you so much. I tell you, I can't go through this again. We'll take care of that"

She looked rather wan, but she was so happy to see her hubby. They talked about their babies. Ashley had not seen them yet. Mark described them to her as best as he could.

The nurse came in to tell them that Ashley needed her sleep now. Ashley's, parents had gone home as soon as they heard that their daughter was going to be just fine. They too had been so worried about their daughter.

Mark's mother would be the twins' pediatrician. They could not be in better hands! Mark was so grateful to her. He would like to phone her, but she needed her rest after this exciting night of rescuing her grandsons and their mother. She was probably sleeping now and she deserved a good rest after saving the lives of three human beings.

Andrew and Colette were overjoyed too, when they saw their daughter the next day. They had worried so much about her. After visiting their daughter and grandsons, they went to Mark's house to make it ready for Ashley and her babies to come home. Colette made several dinners ready to last a few days. With the babies born a month ahead of time everything was not quite ready for the big event of bringing the twins into the house.

Ashley and the boys needed to stay in the hospital for a few more days for further treatment, but they were all three doing very well.

Mrs. Baby Doctor was extremely satisfied with the progress of her two grandsons. All the Maxwells were so happy now that all that worry was behind them. Mark just stood there looking at his two sons and said: "You can just see them growing!"

Of course Ashley was on cloud nine with her priceless little ones and Grandfather Maxwell was so proud of them you'd think that he had made them by hand. The two uncles Sean and James gave Ashley an enormous bouquet and Mark brought her a blooming orchid plant, which she loved and for the boys Papa Mark brought them each a silver mug engraved with their birth date. The names would be engraved later when the decision of their names had been made. It would be quite a while before they could read their names and find out which mug was theirs. However these two did not show any appreciation for this present, as they fell promptly asleep.

After three days the boys were breathing on their own. Their *Dr. Grandmother* was so proud of them. She said they could go home with Ashley in a couple of day's time.

The boys seemed to be truly identical; they were the spitting image of each other. Now the big question of names came up. A lot of names were tried, but they finally decided on Thomas Mark and Robert Andrew: Tommy and Robby. Tommy would be after Ashley's deceased brother and Ashley wanted to keep the name Mark in the family, so Tommy's second name would be after his father, while Robert was the first name of Mark's father and Andrew was Ashley's father's name. Both families were satisfied with the chosen names.

These twins were so alike. How could they keep them apart? After a lot of studying the small guys Ashley found a small mark over the right elbow of the boy with the name tag Robert. One problem was solved: they now knew who Robby was.

The babies were now in Ashley's room for the day. Mark kept holding Ashley as if he was afraid that she would vanish; he had worried so much about her. But his eyes were on the boys.

One day Mark brought his violin and he played a happy tune for his children and their Mom. But did the twins care?

They were pretty good babies, except when feeding time was drawing near, and they would howl their little heads off. Mark tried to soothe them by playing, his violin but they did not seem to want that at all, they wanted to be fed and now!

Of course every one came to take photos and Mark wanted a photo of *Mrs. Baby Doctor* and her grandsons. Everyone was so excited and they all promised to baby sit when needed.

When Ashley came home with her precious little ones she

found out what it was to feed two hungry babies, who wanted their meal at the same time. They also found out that when they changed the boys' diapers they had to keep them covered up if they did not want a wet face.

But someone had forgotten to tell Mark. Ashley laughed so much when she saw Mark's astonished face after the unexpected shower. He said with a smile: "You knew this was coming. I'll make you pay for this!"

Ashley told everyone what had happened. Mark was the butt of a lot of joking.

After Ashley had recuperated from her operation, they had to think of the baptism and they had to choose godparents. They asked Andrew and Mark's mother as well as Sean and his wife, because they were young and could help look after the children's religious and physical health if the parents were not able to do this.

Colette often came over to give Ashley a hand. Also her sisters-in-law were very helpful. Alyson's daughters were only four and eight years old and were so excited to see their new cousins. They were like toy dolls to them and wanted to play with them. At first the babies were not interested at all, but later on as they grew older Ashley promised them that they would be much more fun. Mark often stood by their cradles in awe, looking at his little miracles. Now that they were a little older there were four brownish eyes staring up at him. He noticed that Tommy's eyes were a trifle lighter brown with hazel specks. He had to bring this astounding news immediately to his wife. Now it was Tommy with the lighter eyes and Robby with the mark on his right arm. They were making headway.

The parents were keeping their eyes open for other differences in their traits. Each boy should have his own character, personality and habits. The parents would encourage them to be good human beings and have their own individual manners. They started out with dressing them differently. Mark put a little green shirt on Tommy, while Ashley tried to get a bright red one on the squirming and wriggling Robby.

Again Mark thought he had never seen such wonderful little miracles. Then he played a tune for them, but they did not seem to care. Mark thought after all music needs to be heard several times before it is truly appreciated. He was not discouraged!

Everyone thought this was a joke, but Ashley had an idea that not only was Mark happy playing his violin, but some of the music might enter the boys' little brains.

Of course there were times that the twins cried and cried, upsetting the parents. Several times they were quite hopeless and Mark's mother had to come over and soothe the fears of her son and daughter-in-law. She dutifully examined them and asked them when the last feeding had been. Had they burped? She advised them to let the babies cry for a little while, leave the room, but keep an eye on them.

And indeed but for the usual baby sicknesses, they had not much trouble with the twins. The little boys were the entertainment for them all.

Grandpa Maxwell and Andrew would look into the cribs and they were totally amazed to see these two dark curly heads looking at them. The two men were taught how to tell them apart. When they were allowed to pick them up Andrew took Tommy and Robert Maxwell picked up Robby.

Colette baby sat for her daughter when she had to do her shopping and soon Colette would get more free time when she was retired from teaching in a few weeks time.

Ashley felt much stronger now and was able to play her beloved grand or the violin. She had to keep up practicing these instruments.

On weekends Mark and Ashley put the twins in a double baby carriage and strolled in the park. Occasionally people stopped and peeped inside admiring the dark-eyed boys.

After a few months Tommy and Robby started to enjoy

the attention and one day they discovered each other and tried to grab or touch. They seemed to enjoy being together.

Colette was finishing her last year of teaching and looking forward to being retired, but not from working. She had ideas. After the holidays she was going to write her novel, which had been on her mind for a long time. And then she was planning to see more of her daughter and the twins.

With the summer holidays coming Mark was planning again to direct the Vancouver Festival Orchestra and to travel around on the weekends mainly. They had made up a program which was a real mixture of nearly every kind of music; some oldies or romantic classics, a jazz piece and a little rock and roll to entice the young people. Because of last year's success the agent suggested a couple of weekday concerts in smaller towns as well. The whole orchestra agreed with this idea.

However Ashley was staying home with her boys. They needed all her attention. Mark disliked being away so often, but he arranged coming home as much as possible. Most nights he could fly or drive home.

Advance ticket sales had been very encouraging and the musicians were all enthusiastic about the program. There were quite a few young people in this orchestra. Ashley missed playing with the orchestra, but she would be able to join the group again when the twins were bigger.

This summer Colette wanted to help Ashley so that she could study music and finish writing her book on Music Therapy. She still had to do a little more research, but she had begun the actual writing of the book. All this had to be done in small time periods between feeding, changing, playing with the babies, and going for walks in the park with them.

Colette had been collecting material and ideas for her novel. This last year her mind had been so often on this book. If she thought of some new item she wrote this on a card and filed it alphabetically.

During her twenty- five years of teaching she had experienced many different attitudes and sayings of children, parents and teachers. Some students so often came up with hilarious ideas and sayings, but sometimes there were sad moments too. Many of these observations were recorded in her card system, which now grew by the day since she had more time to spend pondering and remembering certain occasions. In the meantime, she still wrote her poems or musings as she called them. Once she had enough poems her agent had promised to find her a publisher.

Andrew did not want to retire yet, as he enjoyed his work, but he was scaling back a little. He did not take his work home anymore. Maybe the arrival of his grandsons had something to do with that too? There was however not the same spring in his step. He was nearing sixty-five, but he was always ready to visit "his boys".

On weekends, accompanied by Colette, he walked his boys in their baby-carriage. He found them so cute. They started to be really interesting. They were looking at him with their big brown eyes. They were always so happy being pushed around in their pram.

Andrew had a wealth of experience in his field of International law. He discussed this with Colette, who encouraged him to work shorter hours and put his perceptions and knowledge on paper. He agreed that he should start making notes. He also discussed his ideas with Peter, his friend, and colleague who was all for this project. He promised his cooperation and also started to do research on it and making notes. Then again they would discuss their findings. He came over regularly to the Van Heekeren's house to give his input and thoughts. They worked so well together.

After school ended and Colette had retired, Andrew and Colette took a short holiday to Sechelt. Colette needed a rest from the hectic end of the school year activities, such as exams, plays, and other programs which the children had been performing for their parents. Though these activities were enjoyable, they were also very tiring and time consuming.

Whenever they had a chance to go to Sechelt they still looked around for this dream spot, but now that Colette had retired they took a Real Estate agent, who knew of many beautiful lots or maybe he could find them a smaller house.

They started looking around Gibson. There were so many interesting points. Nature at Howe Sound with its fantastic coloring in the early morning: pink and gold on the water with the dark grayish background of Mt. Elphinstone. And the setting sun over Vancouver Island is just magical when the full moon settles over the Strait of Georgia.

Further along on the gravelly coast it is so lovely to see all kinds of large ships as cruise liners, loggers and small fishing boats go past. The harbor with its hundreds of sailboats was interesting to Andrew and Colette, being such avid sailors.

Many cottages and houses are built along the coastal road. Some are nestled into the rocks; some were on top of the rocks overlooking the Strait.

Another interesting part of this Sunshine Coast is the fact that many artists and galleries have settled in Gibson and Sechelt. This too attracted the Van Heekerens. Music festivals and plays are given every summer. Writers come together for seminars here.

Colette in her imagination saw her new yard with bright-colored flowers and flowering shrubs. In this softer marine climate even some tropical plants survive and Colette with her green thumb would make them grow in her garden. Her gardening hobby prevented her from building on rocky terrain. Colette wanted some earth to play with. They did not find what they really wanted in these two weeks of holidays. They decided to return there again in September and stay for another week and eventually drive further north to Pender Bay. In the meantime they kept in touch with the Real Estate Agent.

Colette had started her novel while on holiday and was content with the set up.

However a little kink came in when she saw children playing on the beach. That view was enough to make her want to write another children's book. Her creative artist's brain worked overtime. She told Andrew as they were walking along the coast about her new idea. Andrew laughed heartily. He said: "So this is your view of retiring; you'll be working harder than ever."

She answered: "But writing makes me happy. I can see the story developing as well as the colorful pictures that our friend and illustrator, will make.

She planned pictures for little children; each poem had to have an illustration. Each picture and poem was to be a children's pastime, like playing on the beach, swimming in the sea or the fair with its Ferris wheel, clowns, etc.

Colette felt good; she really had a future. Upon retirement she was making a new beginning, as well as being a new grandmother. Life was so exciting!

She was musing about retirement and wrote:

Musing on Retiring

Retired from an income making employment
So many dreams to fulfill

Never to be looked at as the end
But as the beginning of a new career

Let's be productive with our dreams
We may use the opportunity, time, experience
To solve different kinds of problems

The needy will always be with us,
Therefore much needs to be done in this world.
And what about our own needs?

Journeying through fantastic landscapes
Either in reality or dreams
Opening views to the eyes, mind, and emotions.

Aspiring to all forms of Art, expressed in creativity
Dare to dream
Dare to try out new ideas.

Be curious to discover possibilities
There is no "being bored".
Life is so full of dreams, aims and goals.

Where can we keep growing?
Where can we find inspiration?

But in Nature, while listening to the beat of the thunderous
    ocean
Or enjoying bright flowers and birds in their sanctuaries.

While Colette was away her cleaning lady Minah went to Ashley's place to help out with the boys, so that Ashley could study her instruments without having to worry about Robby and Tommy. Everyone was very satisfied with this arrangement. Minah loved playing with the little babies.

Ashley had been studying the music that Mark was playing with the orchestra. That way she could at any moment fill in for an absent musician.

One day after the rehearsal, Mark came home feverish and feeling poorly. He was sneezing and coughing. Ashley put him straight to bed and phoned her husband's mother. Her mother-in-law said: "Keep him away from the babies. I'll come over first thing in the morning, just give Mark lots of fluids to drink and aspirin. It sounds like the flu."

Poor Mark, he was so hot and miserable and he was not even allowed to see his boys. Early next morning mother Maxwell came over and told her son to stay in bed and "Please stay away from the babies. Be sure to drink a lot."

Mark was worried about the next concert, which was in three days time, but Dr. Maxwell said: "Absolutely not. You have to stay in bed until the fever is down."

Mark was fretting about this, which didn't do him any good. Ashley said: "I'll contact the agent and the concert master." They both agreed that she should take over from Mark. She had all the necessary qualifications to direct an orchestra and she had done enough directing at High School and at the University when she had taught there.

While she thought this over, Mark said: "Of course you can do it."

Colette and Andrew would spend the evening looking after the boys and Mark, who still felt pretty sick. He was so disappointed that he could not see his darling children. But Dr. Maxwell was adamant about this.

One good thing was that the concert was fairly close by in Burnaby and the concert master offered to drive her there. Everything was settled except Ashley's nerves. She got dressed in a simple long navy dress with some beads embroidered around the neckline.

There had only been time for one rehearsal, which went very well. Off she went with the good wishes of husband and parents with her violin case in hand. Mark encouragingly said: "You'll do very well, just remember to go with the music and you will have the orchestra as well as the audience in your hand."

Indeed, as soon as she came on stage she felt the public, who had expected Mark to conduct, were curious and upbeat. Not too many had heard or seen a young female conductor.

The concert master explained that Dr. Mark Maxwell could not be present because of illness, but his wife, another Dr. Maxwell would take the baton. Ashley was nervous, but in her mind she heard Mark saying: "Smile and impress them".

She came on stage with a long confident stride, a big grin on her face and baton in hand. Then with a fast beat of the baton the concert started. No outward sign of nervousness was visible; she was a real trooper. From that first moment on, people appeared to be spellbound. Energy seemed to flow from her to the musicians to the audience. The orchestra started off with a lively march, which kept the audience tapping and in a buoyant mood. Then she turned around and said: "After this exciting music we want to give you a rest to listen and meditate with Massenet's "Meditation."

Facing the audience she showed that total emotion that this music gave her, bringing this feeling over to the public. Success!

CHAPTER 12

September had arrived again and the holidays were over. Mark went back to his regular job of teaching at the University as well as directing the regular concerts of the Vancouver Symphony until the actual conductor Ken Ashton would return.

After a few months it became clear that this would not happen for a long time, if ever. Ken felt well enough to attend a concert sitting in a wheelchair, but he did not have the stamina to stand for nearly two hours.

Ashton suggested that Mark Maxwell be appointed as the conductor. Discussing all this with the Symphony Orchestra board members and musicians Ken Ashton defended Mark by saying: "When you look over the audience you see a sea of grey hair. Couldn't we try to influence the taste of the younger generation by playing a little lighter music? More over aren't we losing money with the Symphony as it is now?"In the end it was decided to go along with Mark's choices. When they discussed the program, Ken suggested that any alterations Mark wanted should be done slowly. Mark agreed to do all changes gradually.

Mark accepted this position and started working with his friend and concert master on programs for the monthly concerts during the winter season. At first they changed very little as the regular concert goers expected classical music, but John and Mark decided to sneak in here and there a lighter, happy overture of a classical nature. Not all the musicians agreed at first but after some give and take from both sides it was decided that the orchestra would play a few lighter and happier classics alternated with their usual high brow masterpieces. They hoped this program would be more attractive to the public in general.

Ken Ashton the former conductor attended the first concert of the season. He was wheeled in by his son.

After the opening of the concert with the "Fifth Symphony" by Ludwig Van Beethoven, Mark addressed the audience saying: "Our former conductor Ken Ashton has recovered enough to be present tonight. We want to thank you Ken for the leadership and devotion you have given to this orchestra for so many years. We all wish you a full recovery."

Between the different pieces of music Mark turned around and either explained the next item on the program or told a short story about the composer or even a quip or wisecrack, just as he was used to doing with his students. Of course he was not hard to look at with his tall figure of six foot two and his curly black hair. Listening to the applause and bravos the concert was a success.

Mark's family attended this first concert as well as Ashley and her parents. Ashley's trustworthy helper was babysitting the twins. Normally they would all go out for a drink after the performance, but circumstances had changed. Ashley wanted to go home to her boys. They all decided to go to Mark's house and celebrate the success of this concert.

As it was feeding time, the boys were diapered, and fed and then traveled from one adoring grandparent to the other.

The whole family was excited about Mark's concert. Everyone had enjoyed it. Even the critics in the papers gave excellent reports about the new conductor.

Ashley's book about music therapy was nearly finished and most of it had been edited by colleagues (music profs. at the U). Her colleagues had corrected, discussed and changed the text as is usual while they were editing. On the whole they were satisfied with the research. Ashley wanted to go over the whole book once more and make sure that everything made sense. This final review would take a couple of weeks. Then to the publisher would go the book!

CHAPTER 13

When Colette started her writing in the morning (before any housework) she chose some CD's, mostly quiet classical music as: Tchaikovsky's music, which was her favorite. She also liked Beethoven's piano sonatas. This music was soothing to her and she could write with that kind of music. She also loved light music of the operettas, like the *Gypsy Baron* and sometimes she appreciated Strauss waltzes or Joplin's upbeat composition as for instance the "Entertainer" or Sondheim's "Send in the Clowns".

This last song inspired her to write a really happy children's story. Ideas for her novel were forever crowding around in her head and she made copious notes of these.

While she was babysitting, she wrote when her little grandsons were asleep. Now they were demanding more attention and wanted to be entertained. Colette loved playing with them. Colette sometimes put the two together in one crib and later in the playpen. The children discovered each other. Colette thought I wished that I could know their feelings for each other??

While playing with the boys she thought of stories she could tell them when they got older. She was convinced that they would love her stories. As soon as possible she wrote those stories down.

Colette felt very lucky to have a family who could understand that she required time and peace. But then being artists themselves they recognized that feeling or need. She was fortunate to be able to discuss her thoughts and ideas with Andrew, who was so easy to talk with. He looked at things from a totally different, dryer viewpoint. His concepts and notions gave her sometimes an entirely different slant to her way of thinking.

Her novel was for a large part set in Ireland. Colette and Andrew had visited this beautiful green country some years ago. They had just loved being there. It might be a good idea to go there *next* spring for a holiday. Andrew would love that too. Her sister-in-law Maeve was Irish and she could advise them where to go and maybe rent a cottage for them with a pretty view of the Atlantic or one of the inlets.

They could soak up some atmosphere and influence of the area and perhaps they could find out about some of the legends and visit the region in which her novel was situated. She had done research on Ireland and made notes. Her laptop came in handy for this.

Since she was now retired she should have more time to play piano too. While teaching music at school she always played what was needed for her classes. Now she could and should take time every day to play. She was going to start with some easy sonatas. She found her mother's old piano books. When she saw the music, such as the "Hungarian Rhapsody" by Liszt, that she had played at sixteen years of age, she knew that she had regressed and needed a lot of study to catch up to that level again. She planned to set aside at least half an hour each day to practice.

After two hours of writing and half an hour of piano playing, it was about time to see her grandsons and give Ashley some time for her book and studying the piano or violin. If the weather was decent she took the boys in the baby-carriage to give them an outing and some fresh air. They loved the movement of the carriage. They either fell asleep or looked around with their big, dark eyes. Soon they would be able to sit up and observe the world around them.

As soon as they came home Colette made lunch for Ashley and herself, while her daughter diapered and fed the babies.

On the way home Colette shopped for groceries and prepared dinner for the two of them.

They attended every concert Mark directed and where their daughter substituted for the absent pianist or violinist. After the concert they all met at Mark's house for coffee and dessert. The baby sitter could go home then in good time. Ashley now had two helpers (Asha and Asita) who earned their University fees by working at Ashley's. They cleaned and cooked and looked after the babies, whenever they were needed. Even the girls' mother, Minah, who helped Colette out, came over if the girls were too busy. This was a wonderful arrangement for all. They needed two more years at the University.

Family gatherings were still happening but most often they went to either of the parents' house and brought the twins along. All four grandparents loved them to pieces and the children were becoming such little characters. This was a true close-knit family. The little ones too seemed to enjoy the visits with their grandparents, who were so proud of them. Mark's brothers' girls saw the babies as their dolls. They loved playing with them. They each took one little boy to play with.

Colette noticed that the twins wanted to be together. They reached for each other. Often when she was observing or playing with the boys, Colette would get an idea for a children's story or poem. These children were a source of inspiration for her and during one of her conversations with Mark she found that her son-in-law was in the same boat. He told her that he would often play or compose while observing his sons or his wife playing with the twins. He said: "Isn't it strange where those creative feelings and ideas come from?"

Sharing and giving were going to be some important new words or rather new ideas for the twins. It took some time to get that idea through to the twins' little heads, but as they matured a little and with a lot of patience Ashley and Colette succeeded a little better as the days went by.

When they started to recognize their toys, they chose different ones, even though there was two of each. After some time it was Robby who decided he wanted the schnauzer and Tommy reached for the lamb, which he held tightly in his little arms. They played with other toys, but Robby held his doggie in one arm while playing with other toys or animals. And strangely enough Tommy did the same, holding on to his lamb.

In between her busy practice, Grandma Maxwell often popped in to see her grandchildren, while they were awake. She tried to make this a habit at least twice a week. The twins started to recognize her now and gave her a big smile and stretched out their arms to be picked up. But how could she pick up two at the same time? Ashley made sure that both came into grandma's arms.

Grandma told them how precious and beautiful and clever they were. They answered back with gurgling noises.

Christmas that year was such a busy time. Both grandparents wanted to have Mark's little family over. They all compromised: all the Maxwells and Ashley's parents came to Christmas dinner at Mark's place. Each family brought dishes, while Colette made the turkey at Ashley's house. At the Dutch bakery she had bought two large Christmas Rings, which were filled with almond spice and decorated with holly leaves made from icing sugar and candied red cherries.

After church they all came to Mark's house. Sean's children entertained and in turn were amused by the twins. Many photos were taken of the boys and Sean's little girls.

These twins received a lot of Christmas presents, but did they care? Who knows? At least they smiled and gurgled at all the faces hanging over the playpen.

Ashley planned to have dinner while the boys had their

naps and for once they cooperated. Most likely they were exhausted. Later there was some caroling. The little nieces and their mother sang their carols first.

Colette played the piano, accompanied by the young couple on their violins and as a surprise Andrew had brought his flute. Andrew seldom played, but he remembered the Christmas Carols.

January and February were miserably cold and wet bringing colds and coughs to many people. With so many people sick Ashley had to substitute several times at the symphony.

Better weather was coming and plans for the trip to Ireland were finalized. Andrew and Colette left May first and rented a car in Dublin. The first day they explored the city and were trying to get used to cars driving on the wrong side of the road.

They visited Waterford and the crystal factory where they ordered several crystal pieces such as a clock and whiskey glasses for friends and family which were to be packed and sent to their address in Vancouver. This had now taken care of most of their shopping for family and friends, except for their grandchildren. They were still looking for safe toy leprechauns. Then on they went to Cork and visited Mizen Head, back to Limerick and Galway, where Maeve had found a cottage along the inlet. Here they rested and actually got to know and understand the Irish people and their culture and folklore, by going to pubs, stores and museums, where they talked and asked questions. Everyone seemed more than willing to explain. The owners of their little cottage gave them a lot of information. They sent them to a bookstore and library with a list of informative titles, to theatres, where they enjoyed dances and plays. They also bought DVDs and CDs of folksongs, and/or Irish orchestras with pipes and fiddles, as well as photos of the different instruments they used.

They visited castles and were told "faery" tales in the pubs and Colette made lots of notes on her laptop and described her ideas and views of this area.

It was so peaceful. The view from their cottage was on the forever changing water of the inlet.

To Andrew the most striking feature of Ireland was the sharp fresh greenness of the area.

After their walks Colette sat down to work out her notes and Andrew read a book, but she noticed that most of the time he fell into a deep sleep for a couple of hours.

She asked him if he was overtired but he always knew how to set her mind at peace. "I feel fine, I am just relaxing."

Much, much later this scene would come back to her.

Colette listened to quite a few legends about beautiful maidens who met princes in the mist as they walked on the beach and some never came back. They had such an interesting time and Colette got loads of ideas and notes for her novel. They had loved going to Pubs, although they found a pint of Guinness an acquired taste.

She heard a story of an ugly witch, who was so jealous of this particularly beautiful young maiden that she turned her into a girl with long ugly teeth and a bulbous nose, so that no young man looked at her a second time. Colette would probably find a happy ending to that story.

They heard tales of evil spirits and faeries living in castles or in ruins of towers and how people could be lured away and kept prisoners for one hundred years. Everything was told with lots of humor and laughter. They listened to Celtic music in the pubs where they heard some heart-breaking songs.

They had enjoyed themselves so much. The holiday was over too soon. They went home with little toys for their grandsons and Sean's children.

Everyone was happy to see them back. The parcel from Waterford had not arrived yet, but these presents were for the grown-ups, who could wait a week or so.

Colette took up her usual routine of writing for two hours

in the morning, playing piano and helping her daughter with the twins. She needed to organize her holiday notes first; her writing was coming along well. Andrew went back to work, but not with the same enthusiasm as before. Colette became a little worried and asked him to see his doctor, and have a checkup. After a long speech of how well he was, he finally saw his doctor, who did not see much wrong with him. His blood pressure was a little high but that could be lowered with some pills and his cholesterol was a little high but if he minded his diet that would improve too. Now Colette had to be satisfied.

Andrew was going to have an important birthday. With the help of Ashley's two faithful student-helpers and of course her Mom they made it a real party. All the Maxwells came as well as their friend Peter. The dinner was delicious. Andrew stood up and made his "Thank you" speech. Then he came out with a totally unexpected announcement: "I have decided to retire and start doing what I feel like doing and when and how. I am now set for freedom and enjoyment. A while ago Colette mentioned that I should write some of my experiences and adventures in the field of law. Since then I have been thinking and actually made a start by writing notes and happenings as they came into my mind. I hope Robert (Mark's father) will have a chuckle here and there. Peter and I have been discussing this and we plan to work together on this project."

Everyone congratulated Andrew with his decision.

Peter who was nearly the same age as Andrew, was not retiring yet as he had no real plans. He agreed that something should be written on that particular area of the law; that is with regard to International Law, this being the department in which both Peter and Andrew worked. More attention should be paid to the moral, constitutional areas; as well as guidelines to implement changes needed to be improved and updated with a more globalised view point.

When it was feeding time for the babies they were handed

around and played with. They all loved this, especially the little boys, who just took in all the attention.

Robert took his namesake and called the poor little fellow "lawyer". Andrew had hold of Tommy and named him "architect." They were all wondering how this would work out. They appeared to be wrong as time would tell. The two men brought the little guys back to bed and reported that they were asleep in no time. No doubt they were tuckered out from all the handling and visiting with everyone.

Ashley's book was approved and published at the University. The Music Department profs found the book of such quality that they made it one of the texts in the music department. It would be available next September at the University bookstore.

In the acknowledgements Ashley thanked her husband for his cooperation and patience with her and her mother for the scrupulous editing of the book. Ashley gave a complimentary book to her parents, the Maxwells and Peter of course, as he had become practically a member of the family. He seemed to need that relationship with the Van Heekerens, but he tried not to depend upon them too much. Being an only child and no longer having parents or a wife, he was often very lonely. Colette and Andrew noticed that and encouraged Peter to travel and see what else there was in this world.

Colette suggested meetings with people in other countries in the field of International law. Indeed he heard her and made several appointments in France, England and Holland, which has that beautiful Peace Palace in The Hague. Now he had a purpose and what a difference that made. He had not dared to retire, because he was afraid to get bored when he had nothing to do. Now he prepared for his pension and organized several tours and appointments in The Hague via the Dutch consulate in Vancouver, as well as in Paris and Switzerland.

After his retirement he stayed away for three months, exploring and admiring the different landscapes and observing the various cultures as well as meeting the contacts that the three consulates had advised to see.

He came back a new man, full of spirit and humorous stories. Andrew and Peter now had so much to discuss and to work on. Within these three months he had totally changed in attitude and outlook on life. Andrew and Colette could not believe that this was the same man, who had mourned the loss of his wife for so long.

CHAPTER 14

Now that the book on Music Therapy was out of the way Ashley could thoroughly enjoy her babies' antics and pay attention to their progress. She started to see differences between the twins. When sitting on her lap they could touch the piano keys and hear what they did. One of them, Tommy seemed more interested in the sound he had made. Robert hit any old way. Mama Ashley tried to show him to hit one note and listen; he just laughed and hit wildly, while Tommy listened intently. He seemed excited about the sound one key made and then tried another. He sat on Ashley's lap playing that way for a long time, while Robert was off and romping around, touching whatever toys he could reach.

The room had been made childproof. Every little thing was now either in cupboards or high up so that the children could not reach any precious article. Everything was a toy to them. The boys were now in the process of trying to walk and climb. They had oodles of fun, trying out everything and in the meantime, keeping Mom busy teaching and helping them.

Tommy also listened carefully when Mark played his violin. He enjoyed Mark's playing. Sometimes he climbed on his Mom's lap while she was playing the piano and Mark accompanied her on his violin. He just sat there quietly. His attention span was astonishing for his age.

Not Robert, he was off in no time, playing with his toys.

It looked as if he wanted to play mostly with his blocks. His parents bought him an extra set of blocks so that he could build more with them.

Mark and Ashley were happy to see that each child was gearing up to diverse pursuits. Sometimes they played and quarreled together. Robert wanted to build only his way. Mama Ashley had to bring peace and teach them the word "sharing."

Ashley had now a little more time to substitute at the Symphony. She really enjoyed playing with Mark at home and also with the musicians. They were such a wonderful group of people. They all believed in the magic and bewitchment of music.

During rehearsals Mark sometimes sat in the middle of the hall listening how certain sounds or renditions would be heard at that distance. The acoustics were generally pretty good, but sometimes he would make a change in the playing or seating of the musicians. While Mark was listening Ashley took over the conducting. That way she kept up to date in that department and she loved that.

They found their group of musicians harmonious, maybe because music gives a certain kind of peace. There is no difference in color, race, religion, nationality, or language in music. What counts is whether it gives a message. It could be boisterous, rhythmic or sad, but it must be harmonious. The *Sister Act* gives such an example.

Mark and Ashley felt so strongly about that. In music one may have unreachable dreams. They believed in the magical powers of dreams and music. Music gives way to many emotions as sadness, cheerfulness, sympathy, but also respect and enchantment. It is no miracle that babies fall asleep on the soft, soothing melody of lullabies.

Music binds people together, as Schiller says: "All men will be brothers." Music and love will do that.

Ashlcy showed in her book on music therapy that music

may help students with reading and mathematics when soft music is played in the background. Attention span seemed to improve as well.

Not only does music express quiet and peace, but it may show war, death, strife and haunting as in the films about the Civil War depending on how this music is played, it may bring happiness, concern, emotion and joy, giving confidence to the future.

All this was so important to Ashley and she found in Mark a ready music lover and partner in crime, who perceived atmosphere and sensations from music, while bringing this over to the audience. No words are needed when music goes deep into the heart of people who are appreciative and open to listening. A willingness to listen is a prerequisite needed in so many aspects of life.

Often enough though words are important and bring extra meaning which is shown with choirs. Here the art of writers comes into play.

Also nature goes hand in hand with music.

Mark and Ashley enjoyed walking with the boys in Stanley Park. They loved the views from the beach. They tried to show the boys birds and flowers, water and boats. The twins were beginning to be curious and needed to find out about everything they saw. Birds must have been fascinating to them as they always pointed to the sky.

The boys had now started to chatter, which was not always understandable to the grown-ups, but they seemed to know what the other was saying.

They had their childhood colds and were miserable, which made their parents unhappy. They often got sick at the same time. Then Ashley did not have enough hands to soothe them and take care of them, which made her feel so wretched as well.

CHAPTER 15

Colette found writing such a challenge as well as inspiring. So many faculties can be used in this occupation. It is like a symphony; there is a mixture of psychology, philosophy, sociology and even mythology could be thrown into writing a novel or poem.

She was living in her characters. Then there was the English language. Colette liked the sound of words, playing with word-sounds and meanings. She thoroughly enjoyed writing her novel.

Since Andrew was home now, they would both work for a couple of hours in the morning and after coffee they either visited Ashley and saw their grandsons or took the boys out in the baby carriage for a long walk, which they all totally enjoyed. Now the twins were so interested in their surroundings and they pointed to, for them interesting things, such as birds or people.

Andrew had become very involved in his project on a certain part of International law. He worked with Peter on this. Peter, who had also worked with Andrew at the Justice Department, came over often for discussions and clarifications. He had brought a lot of information and impressions home from his trip to Europe. His viewpoint had widened. They enjoyed working together as they had always done at the department. They had many discussions on International Law that had to do with Immigration and its liabilities, rights and moral implications.

Actually not too much had changed for them except that they were doing what they wanted to do and when. They also liked taking their own time and place to do it. Was this called "work"? They liked unraveling these new ideas.

One night Andrew woke up Colette. She saw immediately Andrew was in deep trouble. He could not breathe. He was in excruciating pain and was sweating heavily. He just managed to say: "Call for an ambulance."

Colette phoned and jumped into her slacks and sweater. The emergency crew did what was needed, but Colette saw that Andrew was in great danger. Colette prayed and prayed, which was all she could do for him. She could see Andrew suffering and actually leaving her.

As soon as they arrived at the hospital Colette phoned Ashley, who said that she was on her way. However it was too late. Andrew, her beloved father had passed away. It all had happened so quickly. Everyone was in shock, especially Colette.

Mark brought the boys to his brother, Sean's house and came to the hospital as soon as possible. It was all so incomprehensible!

Colette stayed with Ashley and Mark until after the funeral. The little boys gave her something else to think about beside Andrew's death.

There was a large funeral with a High Mass and many former colleagues and friends attended.

The day after the funeral Colette went to her own apartment, she said: "I have to learn to live alone and I will make it. Andrew will be proud of me. But I am so lonely without him."

Then again she whispered: "How selfish I am, would I want him to live and suffer as I saw him going through that terrible pain? He is in a better place now."

However even that thought did not help her too much.

Peter was a big help. He organized all the estate administration for her and took her to her lawyer, organized the death certificate and widow's pension. He helped her to get rid of Andrew's possessions and clothing. He now took care of her as she and Andrew had done for Peter when his wife Marion had died.

Colette had a hard time; she missed her best friend and dear husband. Every time she had an idea she wanted to discuss, she discovered that she was talking to no one. Going to that large bed alone was an experience she did not wish on anyone.

As other couples they did not always agree but they had promised before their marriage to make up their differences before going to sleep. There certainly was no need for that anymore.

Peter often came over in the evenings as Colette found the hours after supper very long. He had taken home most of Andrew's notes and papers regarding their book they had been writing. As Andrew had often discussed this work with Colette, she happened to know quite a bit about this undertaking and Andrew's way of thinking. Peter continued these discussions with Colette too. He took her out to dinner once or twice a week and she occasionally went out with some former colleagues and friends.

Her days were filled with her usual writing in the morning. At first she did not feel like writing at all. Her mind was not clear enough for that, but after a couple of weeks she told herself that nothing would change the situation. Andrew was gone, she now had to make a life for herself; like it or not! Andrew would have wanted her to get on with her life and make the best of it.

Her religion helped her somewhat and the fact that Andrew did not have to suffer for very long. It could have been worse. She knew Andrew expected her to make the best of the situation. Easier said than done!

But she did it and nobody needed to know that she had a good cry now and then. But Colette knew she could be strong. She had experienced the loss of their son Tom. However at that time she leaned on Andrew and Andrew supported her, which made an enormous difference. Even though it was hard for her to see how much the death of Tom had affected Andrew at that sad time.

Colette put on a good show for Ashley and Mark. That the boys were becoming such funny little creatures helped a lot. They always gave her a big grin and tried to say: "Grandma."

Mark and Ashley were getting on with their life in the music world and being occupied with their twins. Robby could keep busy for a long time with his blocks and building things. He had the ability and steady hands to stack blocks and other toys on top of each other. But not Tommy he played for a little while with his brother and then asked with gestures to be allowed to touch the piano. He knew he had to have his hands washed before he touched the piano. For touching the piano he would even agree to have his hands wiped, and normally he did not like this. He never banged or hit the keys hard.

When Ashley was playing most of the time he would just look at her fingers moving so fast over the keyboard and one would say he was in awe of her performance.

Colette got such a kick out of observing the little fellows. The twins unknowingly helped the grown-ups to get over their sorrow with their antics and naughtiness.

Mark and Ashley being true musicians went back to their playing. Especially Mark, who was so sensitive, drowned his sadness in music. He had really loved and respected his father-in-law. When Ashley was playing the piano he could hear her sadness and said sometimes: "Let's play some happy music for the boys."

Ashley was asked by the Symphony board to become a

regular violinist and substitute pianist as well as substitute conductor. It happened only seldom that Mark had to attend a function or a meeting at the University. But they found it was good to be prepared for all eventualities and Colette encouraged Ashley too by saying: "I will baby sit on rehearsal and symphony nights."

Ashley agreed to this on the condition that if one of her helpers was free to look after the boys on Symphony nights, Mom would then come with Ashley and Mark.

However when Peter heard about this arrangement, he asked if he could drive Colette to the concert. She accepted this offer gladly. They both loved music and on top of it Mark and Ashley were performing! What more could they ask?

The Maxwell's too attended their son and daughter-in-law's concerts. They were all so pleased with Ashley's definite appointment at the Symphony as a violinist. Not too often were husband and wife in the same orchestra. But it had happened before. The conductor of the Philadelphia orchestra was married to his harpist many years ago. Sir Andre Previn married the violinist Anne-Sophie Mutter.

After the concert they all went to Mark's house for a glass of wine and discussion of the music and of course to see the little ones. They were so precious.

Colette's book was coming along slowly because the twins inspired her sometimes to write a children's story, which interrupted writing her novel, because she felt the little story had to be written right then and there at the spur of the moment.

Each person in the family had dealt differently with the loss of Andrew. Colette found strength in her religion and she knew that Andrew was now in a better place and without pain. She tried therefore to accept his death, which was not so easy to do. Mark and Ashley drowned their sorrow in music, but often they reminded each other that for the children's sake they had to keep up their good spirits.

Mark's and Ashley's agent came up with the idea that both should go on the Vancouver Festival Orchestra's summer tour. Indeed they would like to do that, but first they had to organize baby sitters. Colette did not see any difficulty there. If they had to stay overnight in a hotel, Colette could stay with them in the same hotel. "No worries in that department", she said. "The boys are getting to be a little easier to handle and they would be ready for bed before you leave."

Both parents agreed and thought how nice it would be to have the boys with them and in good hands. Colette was such a lovely grandmother to the twins. She loved them, but she was still strict enough too. She had had many years of experience with her schoolchildren, who also needed love and understanding, but obey they had to.

Though the agent organized everything such as concert halls, hotels, etc.; Mark had to set up a program far ahead so that the advertisements and programs could be made up. Again as it was last year it was going to be a light program for the Vancouver Festival Orchestra. Light hearted marches, foot-tapping dances, then a profound emotional-feeling piece of music, which went deep into the heart of the audience.

Ashley thought back to the time when she was teaching band to young people and she remembered the kind of music they enjoyed. This music had to be on the program for the teenagers too. And for the seniors they included several classical pieces, sometimes with a different beat, which was a good experience for all to listen to.

That summer they traveled around a bit with the orchestra, which was good for Colette. She had no chance to sit at home and brood. The little ones either kept her occupied or she would write while the twins slept.

The concert tour was a great success, just as last year's had been. They spent their time at home rehearsing and reviewing the program. Also they had to prepare next season's symphony program. Mark needed to go to the University for meetings and to prepare his classes. He also loved to go out with his boys and show them the birds and animals and flowers. The summer had passed too fast. The boys had started to walk which meant they wanted to get out of the carriage and back in again when they got too tired and out again when they saw something interesting to them.

In between concerts Colette often went out with Peter for meals, which gave them both a chance to discuss their projects. One day he told her that he wanted to go back to The Hague and Switzerland for more information and clarification for his book. He thought he would leave around September 15th. Then he got an idea! And the moment he got that idea, it was out of his mouth.

"How about going too, Colette? You may pick up some ideas for your stories and poems. We could stop for a few days in Ireland, so that you may get some more ideas and impressions for your book. You are editing my book already; you can continue doing that on the trip also. What do you think? It will be a good change for you. There will be different scenery and meeting other people will broaden your horizon."

"I don't know, I have not thought about this. Let me ponder on this a bit and talk it over with Mark and Ashley."

"I have not booked the flight and hotels yet, so I am easy on the dates. Let me know. Ashley and Mark will most likely encourage you to take a break. It will do you good to be away from it all."

Colette thought and discussed this with her daughter and son-in-law. To her surprise they were all for it. Ashley had known Uncle Peter nearly all her life. He and his wife used to go out often with Andrew and Colette and the children. They all loved camping in the wilderness of British Columbia. They thought it would be good for both Peter and Colette. They should not be worrying about what others are thinking or saying. As long as they knew for themselves that they were doing the right thing. Ashley and Mark understood that Colette was missing Andrew still very much and that she often still cried and seemed so sad. They also could see that Peter could get her out of such a mood. It was then decided that Peter would organize the trip, book hotels for two rooms or a suite. Colette suggested that they just go to The Netherlands and Switzerland as it seemed that they would be away for quite awhile. He got in touch with his acquaintances in Holland and Switzerland and made appointments with them.

Peter was able to get an apartment for two weeks in Scheveningen. This was conveniently close to The Hague and transportation was easy, because the tram stopped right in front of their door and went straight down town.

Peter saw the different people he had wanted to meet and he could find the information he needed in the Peace Palace library. They were asked out socially at night several times.

While Peter met his contacts, Colette liked to walk on the beach getting inspiration for her children's stories. On the occasional lovely day there were little ones playing and running in the sand, building dikes around their castles, making deep pits to sit in and be out of the wind.

Colette got some good ideas while she was walking along that noisy, sometimes nearly deafening surf. To warm herself she would go into a coffee house with a view of the beach and surf. She enjoyed the lovely creamy cakes and a good cup of strong coffee. She also picked up a few Dutch words and phrases. And she remembered several Dutch expressions that her mother and father had used. She found it interesting how so much of that language came back to her, especially as she never had a chance to speak Dutch anymore.

Many ideas came to her head of which she made notes as soon as she came to the apartment and sometimes when Peter was away she continued working on her novel. Another day the two of them visited museums, palaces and old buildings as the old prison house and interesting parts of the city. They spent one day in Amsterdam and a day in Rotterdam and

Delft, where they visited the Delft Blue factories. This place was of special interest to Colette because her forefathers had lived and worked as artists in this industry right there in Delft. She bought a beautiful Delft blue lacy plate for Ashley, a Delft blue cheese board for Mrs. Maxwell Sr., and tiles for herself and friends. The factory would send all the articles that they had bought to Vancouver. For the twins she bought boy dolls and for Sean's girls she bought girl dolls. They had such a good and fascinating time. They took away many new ideas. Peter had acquired a lot of material and he felt satisfied about this.

While they were travelling in Holland, Colette thought of setting her next book in this county or maybe a part of the book. In preparation she made numerous notes. What a blessing that she had brought her laptop!

Then they flew to Bern and took a short trip through the Alps and on to Geneva. Here they were planning to stay for two weeks. Peter had rented an apartment overlooking Lake Geneva. It was simply magnificent!

Most of the meetings went smoothly for Peter. He found a lot of information. His friends there were very encouraging and helpful. They agreed that someone should have a good look into this international law problem. They hoped to receive a copy of his book when it was published. Peter left with a heavy bag of books and papers and he was happy about the result of all these meetings.

Colette too had done some work on her novel, but she also walked and rested a lot which she had needed. Now she looked wonderfully fit; quite an improvement of five weeks ago. Before the trip she had looked so wan and withdrawn. By now they were ready to go home and see Ashley, Mark and the twins. Colette had phoned home several times and she had talked to the boys, who had answered in some strange baby language. Anyway it was good to hear them. According to Ashley they would see an immense change in behavior as well as in expressing themselves. Mark said: "They now let you know what they want and when."

Everyone was doing fine. Mark had discovered a promising young piano student. He asked Ashley "Would you like to have a piano student come to the house?" "Oh yes," she said, "I would love to do that if you think she is that good."

Mark made the arrangement and when Ashley heard this young lady play, she was pleasantly surprised. Lisa had a wonderful touch and feeling for music. Ashley thought it would be exciting to teach her. Ashley's free time was filling up, but that's what she wanted anyway.

They all celebrated Colette's and Peter's homecoming. They were so happy to see Colette looking so well. And indeed Colette returned, rested and practically her old happy self. Colette started her usual writing in the mornings, and then visited the twins, who were always excited to see their "gamma".

However after a few days she started to feel lonely again. She knew she had been spoiled by Peter's company. There was nobody to talk to and no one to answer her questions.

After a few days Peter phoned and asked her how she was doing and would she go out to dinner with him? They were actually glad to see each other again. Had they missed each other? Had their friendship grown? Whatever they felt they planned to get together regularly to discuss their writings. May be that was a good enough reason for getting together?

Indeed they were immediately in full swing talking and discussing. Peter was telling her about the notes he had organized. As Andrew had always discussed his ideas, she understood Peter's thoughts and notions. She was editing his book, which Andrew had just started and had discussed with Peter and Colette before his death.

They found that sometimes working or talking at Colette's apartment worked better for them as they had some of Andrew's papers and notes right there.

Peter had become a good cook since he had lived alone for

such a long time. It depended on their mood where they ate. Sometimes Peter accompanied Colette to Ashley's place when she went to baby sit. He loved those little boys too. He had known them since birth. Colette tried to make the twins say "Uncle Peter" but they only succeeded saying what sounded like "eet" and that was enough for the time being.

They made a habit of going for long walks, discussing their writing, story or poem or nature as they saw it. Beach, sea and surf or forest and mountains inspired a new tale, thought, idea or concept.

Finally Colette's novel was finished and sent to her agent, who found a publisher for her but on the condition that she changed a certain viewpoint in the story. The editor pointed out that the story would flow smoother, more fluent.

At first Colette found that change-over hard to do. This was her baby, she could not manage it.

She talked this over with Peter who could see the editor's point of view and he told her very diplomatically how he would like to see it. She let it rest for a while and came back to it with a fresh mind.

After a few days Colette read the corrected part to Peter, who said: "Now the relationship is so much easier to understand, much clearer."

The editor was very pleased with the outcome. The book was going to be published. Colette was delighted. Peter took her out for a celebration dinner. He seemed as happy about this feat as she was.

Later Colette thought Peter is such a caring man; he shows how happy he is for me and my success.

Of course Ashley and Mark were happy for her too. They tried to teach the boys to say: "Congratulations", but they did not get farther than "con". "Happy" was more understandable.

All this took place over several months. They were amazed when three months later Colette received the "Book of the Year

Award" Colette was nearly beside herself. What a reward for all her work!

Peter was so excited; he gave her a big kiss, then pulled back and thought to himself hey that felt good.

Colette too had sensed something. They looked at each other more than a little surprised. They did not comprehend this unfamiliar sensation at that moment. They pulled back and continued their conversation, but later when Peter left, that strange emotion and that look in Peter's eyes came back to her and she wondered what she had seen there. She did not know.

Peter was surprised too, but he was a little faster in understanding because he felt that the kiss was reciprocated, although not really grasped.

He had seen astonishment in her eyes. He himself felt good about that, but he was not so sure about Colette's feelings. This might be too early after Andrew's death. She was still suffering from losing Andrew. He had gone through that experience himself. He knew how it felt when he lost Marion. He thought he would never get over that loss. Actually he never did. He had not been interested in anyone so far until this astonishing moment.

Colette and Peter knew each other so well, they talked about Andrew and Marion and how they would have reacted about certain things. Peter knew that he never could forget Marion, although he was now over the real hurt of his pain and loss. At the present he even had a glimmer of hope and of happiness. But he knew that he would have to go slow with Colette and let their friendship grow into the love he hoped they could achieve. They already had a wonderful friendship that for him had grown into love and respect. Colette was such a fantastic lady with some exceptional creative talents for writing and music. He was really proud of her. He thought about all this and became more convinced that they should become a couple. But now how to go about it?

He wondered whether she would miss him if he left the city for a while. He needed to see some law-Professor in Montreal with regard to his book. Andrew and he had studied under Professor Campbell many years ago. Peter had been in contact with him and Dr. Campbell had suggested that he come over and discuss several issues and get more information.

He mentioned to Colette that he needed to go to Montreal about his book. Colette said: "I'll miss you. Be sure to be back before Christmas."

Peter thought that sounded promising. Peter had a surprise, because even Ashley said: "Come back soon, Peter, we'll all miss you and the boys want to play with you."

Peter was taken aback; he had not thought that the whole family had cared so much for him. And off he went. He wondered, will she notice my absence.

To Colette the days seemed longer, even though she was quite busy. Christmas had to be thought of and presents for the boys, Ashley, Mark, other family members and of course for Peter, had to be bought. She wanted to find something special for him. He had been so good to her and helpful. But what? Finally she found a leather cover with an empty notebook in it and several pockets for notes and a spot to hold a pen. After a search in a specialty shop she discovered a gold Cross pen, which fitted right in the leather notebook cover. She was pleased with this buy. Peter would most likely be writing more books in the future. She was practically sure of that, because he had mentioned several ideas he wanted to research and eventually write about.

Buying presents for her grandsons was easier. They liked things on wheels, moving about and for Tommy she bought a small flute, while Robert's present would be things for drawing, or rather what he thought was drawing pictures.

Colette discovered a beautifully embroidered tablecloth with twelve napkins for Ashley and *Mrs. Baby Dr.* and leather wallets for the men in the family.

With Christmas coming soon, Colette's mind went to Christmas stories for little ones, which she discussed with her artist friend, Caroline. It would be a long time for next Christmas, but publishers like to have their material ready way ahead of that time.

Colette was glad to be so busy, because the evenings were starting to be pretty long. She knew she had been spoiled by Peter's company. In the evenings during their holidays they had always discussed the days' happenings and their writing.

Ashley and Mark were kept busy with their music and any spare time she had, Ashley would be found at the piano or violin.

Often enough, while Colette was looking after the boys she heard her daughter playing Chopin's music, which was her favorite. Her fingers just flew over the piano. And sometimes she would catch Tommy just standing beside Ashley, looking in wonder at her playing.

Colette too played piano at night; sometimes it was dreamy music, while thinking of Andrew and how it used to be with him occasionally accompanying her on the violin or his flute.

Another time she would be thinking of Peter and their holiday together and how kind he was and always ready to help. While thinking of the twins she played happy music.

At this time of the year you could hear Christmas carols everywhere; in the stores and in the malls. While she was playing these, she thought maybe I should go to the nursing home and see if they could use my talent there. May be the church choir could use my playing. It proved that both organizations needed her badly. She really would be busy until December 25th. After that she hoped that Peter would be around.

All presents were wrapped and Colette was just getting ready to play the organ at Midnight Mass, when there was a knock on the door. She looked through the peephole and was she stunned! She fumbled with the locks, while calling out: "Peter, you're here!"

She fell into his open arms. They were both shocked by this. Peter kissed her and the kiss was returned, which astonished them both. They started talking at the same time, and then sat down on the couch side by side. Peter told her that he had returned just a couple of hours ago and he had wanted to surprise her. He certainly succeeded in this!

After making fresh coffee with cake, she told him that she had to play the organ at the church for Midnight Mass. He said: "Fine, I'll go with you."

"But you must be so tired after that long flight."

He said, "Yes, a little, but not enough to miss your playing. I don't play an instrument, but I enjoy most kinds of music."

They walked to the church arm in arm, against a strong wind. The service was quite impressive and the music was beautiful. The choir and organist performed so well that many of the church goers were affected deeply by the musical production.

Colette phoned Ashley to tell her that Peter had returned from his trip. Ashley promised to phone Peter to invite him for Christmas dinner with all the Maxwells.

Ashley said to Mark: "Mom seems to be more than happy that Peter is back. I wonder if that tells us something and whether she knows herself how important Peter has become in her life?"

Mark agreed, saying: "Peter knows what he is doing and I cannot blame him, Colette is a wonderful, good-looking woman. They have known each other over thirty years. Didn't Peter go to Law school with Andrew?"

"Yes, Peter and Marion went camping in their own trailer, and came along with us, as long as I can remember. Peter came with our family even after Marion had died. Dad always encouraged him to join us. Peter seemed to like our family's company and Tom often stayed at his trailer to give the three of us more room."

Christmas dinner was a great success. Everyone had

brought a dish. Ashley had cooked a gigantic turkey. Everyone had come loaded with presents. Sean's girls were so excited and not only with unwrapping their parcels, but they loved to play with Tommy and Robby, who had a great time tearing paper off their presents. For a while it looked like a free for all; the little boys went wild, encouraged by their cousins.

Ashley fed the twins early and put them to bed, they were exhausted from all this excitement. The grown-ups managed to enjoy their dinner in peace as the little girls were rather well behaved.

After all had left, Ashley asked Mark: "Well, what do you think?"

Mark replied laughingly: "I suppose you are talking about Peter and your Mom? Yes, Peter is definitely in love with Colette. His eyes follow her everywhere. Colette likes him very much but I am afraid that she will fight that feeling within herself; I don't think she knows yet that she loves Peter. She will get a shock when she finds out. It will be hard for her as she will remember her love for Andrew. We will have to stand by her."

Ashley agreed, but for now they had to leave it up to Peter and his diplomacy and patience.

Indeed Peter advanced very slowly, very carefully. He came over nearly every day, but occasionally he stayed away a day or two as he said, he was working on his book and he had meetings with some law-professors and members of the law society. Returning after a few days he told her that he had missed her so much.

It had been decided to make Peter and Andrew's book into a text book. Peter sent it finally to the University Press. He had dedicated the book to his best friend, Dr. Andrew Van Heekeren, who had been the co-author until his death.

Peter brought a copy of the book home for Colette, who burst out in tears when she read the dedication and the title page with both Andrew's and Peter's name as authors. She thanked Peter and kissed him, which was something Peter liked very much. But he was still very careful. He felt he had to go slowly with Colette and did not go any further. It was still too soon for her after Andrew's death. She would not be ready for a commitment.

Sometimes they took Colette's grandchildren out for a walk. Peter liked that too and the boys loved being with Peter, who would play a little rougher with them than their grandma. They enjoyed trying to catch him. They laughed and yelled, their little legs pumping as they ran and sometimes fell, and then needed to be cuddled or the hurt had to be kissed better.

Colette often thought what a shame that he never had children. He just loves them so much. He is like a child with them. What a good man he is! And I am so lucky to have him as a friend or rather he is better than a friend."

One day Peter came over and Colette could see immediately that something had happened, he was so excited! "Will you believe this? I have unexpectedly inherited a house in Horseshoe Bay with a view of the Bay. Here is a letter from my step-aunt's lawyer. I did not even know this aunt. My parents never talked about her. Something must have happened in the family a long time ago. And now there is no one left to ask questions. I have an appointment with this lawyer tomorrow morning. He will organize my taking possession of the house and give me the keys. Will you come with me, Colette?"

She thought that maybe it should be a more private meeting with the lawyer. He may have some private business to discuss.

But Peter insisted. "You are my closest family. I want to share this with you."

Colette agreed. The lawyer told them where the house was. He gave Peter the keys and another surprise: a bank account of $ 100 000 which was left after funeral expenses, lawyer fees, housekeeper's salary and pension had been paid. Everything was paid for.

The lawyer could not tell Peter much about the aunt, only that she had lived quietly in her small house with her faithful housekeeper. She had contacted him about a year ago and she made her will with his help.

The aunt had not wanted to be in contact with Peter, but she had been curious enough to want to know what kind of person Peter, the son of her stepbrother, was. She had the lawyer find out his background and achievements. Evidently she was satisfied and willed him the house and investments.

That afternoon Peter and Colette went to have a look at Peter's inheritance. They were pleasantly surprised. The brick bungalow was in immaculate condition as well as the yard, which had the most beautiful flowers. Colette was especially drawn to the many different kinds of roses. The house had three bedrooms, a smaller kitchen, but a large living room, a good sized dining room and a lovely sunroom, which was insulated and the view from here was spectacular, overlooking the bay and all its shipping traffic.

The house was built in 1920, but it had been modernized. A second bathroom had been put in and everything was on the ground floor. The aunt had organized this house for the comfort of an elderly lady like herself. There were no steps anywhere in the house.

The housekeeper was there to greet them and explain the workings of the house and yard. She explained that his Aunt had taken care of her future and expressed her thankfulness for this. She would be moving out the next day to live with her sister. She told them that there had always been a gardener once a week for mowing and trimming.

Peter asked her to keep him on so that the garden would stay in the same perfect condition. When the housekeeper had left them, Peter and Colette sat on the couch in the pleasant living room for a while, discussing Peter's luck and several of the lovely aspects of the house; the antiques, the furniture, the view, the garden. Peter said suddenly: "Colette wouldn't you like to live here?"

She looked at him in total amazement. She said, "Yes, it is a lovely house."

"But would you like to live here with me?"

This shocked her even more. She looked at him. She was startled and confused. She just did not understand what he really said.

Peter laughed at himself and said: "That did not come out too well. Let me start again and at the beginning. I have always enjoyed your company and friendship, but for quite a while now I have been wanting more than your care and friendship. I found I want to be with you all the time." Then he hesitated: "To be honest, I love you Colette and I think you care for me."

Colette looked up at him, startled! Then a light went up in her eyes. She suddenly understood what had been bothering her.

She said: "Yes, I know now what has been happening to me. But Andrew..... Peter knew what was going on in her mind. He said: "You won't love Andrew any less. I understand you. You have loved Andrew and cared for him so long, but he is gone and he would not want you to be alone and unhappy. He'll be the first to say: "If you think you can be happy with Peter, go for it." And don't you think we could be happy together? You do care for me, don't you? You need not forget Andrew. As a matter of fact, we'll be talking about Andrew and remembering the things he used to do. He was my best friend."

"Colette, these last few months have been very strange for me too. I always liked you and regarded you as my best friend's wife.1 admired and respected you and what you stood for; your writing, your music, your love for Andrew and your daughter and grandchildren. I think that the trip to Europe brought a change into my way of thinking. Our conversations grew in depth. You have such a profound feeling for life and nature, as you had for Andrew and I valued that and my feelings for you grew."

"You don't need to answer immediately. Why don't you think this over, see how you get used to the idea and your feelings for me. We are not going to cut Andrew out of your life, nor out of mine. I think we will have a good life together. We enjoy many of the same things. And I love you Colette."

Colette said that she liked him and respected all he stood for and indeed there was more in her feelings for him. She said: "I would like to think this through, because the idea is so new to me."

"Thanks," Peter said, "that's all I want you to do right now. Think about it and be sure that I love you and want to live with you for the rest of our lives."

Colette then mentioned Ashley. But Peter was ready with his answer: "I would not be surprised if Mark and Ashley did not have an inkling of an idea of what is going on in my mind. I am practically sure that they sense my feelings for you. Moreover they love you so much they want you to be happy."

Colette was overwhelmed. Peter took her in his arms, kissed her and said: "Take your time making up your mind. Whatever you decide, we will remain friends. Whatever decision you make I'm going to have a piano put in here for you. You must have that instrument whenever you are here. I enjoy your playing so much."

Peter brought Colette home. She was still rather fuzzy and mixed up. That night she went to see Ashley and Mark to discuss her predicament. But things went easier than she had expected. She even had an idea that Mark and Ashley did not think this idea so strange. It was as if they anticipated this. When she asked them their opinion, Ashley said: "Mum, we could see how fond Peter is of you. And we only want the best for you. Don't worry about what others will be saying.

We know that Dad would not want you to mourn forever. He loved you and wants you to be happy. And Peter would be Dad's first choice for you."

Peter was going to be busy for a few days organizing the sale of his condo. He hoped to move soon into the inherited house in Horseshoe Bay. This would give Colette a little time to think and as Peter hoped to miss him. And indeed she thought a lot about him and even more than she had expected. When he wasn't around she wondered what he was doing.

What a quandary she was in! Her heart was saying: "He loves me. I can see that easily. He always was so kind and giving and especially since Andrew's death." She was still hurting from the loss of Andrew but her thoughts were so often of Peter. He loves Ashley and the twins. He had been such a close friend of Andrew and Andrew had thought that Peter was his best friend.

Then again she thought it's too soon.

Her heart argued I love that man.

And in her mind she went on: "This is a different kind of love! More mature! I do not love Andrew less. There is a new joy in Peter's love. There are so many different kinds of love to give as in loving her daughter Ashley and her little boys."

Thinking again of Peter, it came to her suddenly that Peter was all alone in this world. There was not one family member left. Colette now understood why he loved going to Ashley's house. He was so fond of the twins. She thought about this for a day or two.

Then meditating upon all this her mind came to the idea of how happy she could make Peter and that he could have a family now for which he had longed for. Yes, she thought, I will marry him and try to make him happy.

She could actually see Peter's face as it was portraying his love. This made up her mind. To love and be loved could be hers if she said the words.

She knew Peter was so busy, but somehow she was convinced that he would not be too busy for her. She phoned him and asked if she could come over, but he suggested that he would come to her place as he had started packing and organizing for the move and it was rather an upheaval in his apartment.

He was at Colette's apartment in fifteen minutes.

"How did you get here so fast?"

"I flew. I knew that you would not have phoned me unless it was urgent. And here I am. What is it?"

That rush to come over was enough for Colette to know how much he cared for her. She was now sure of his love and hers. The expression on her face must have given her away. He took her in his arms and danced around with her.

"I take it that you agree that we belong together."

There had been uncertainty indeed, but now she saw love in his face and she answered his longing with a spontaneous: "Yes, I love you."

There would be joys, but also fears, which they could overcome together. It was rather late that night when Peter left, but early the next morning, a large bouquet of rose-tipped white roses arrived. Colette knew what that meant. A while ago they had discussed John O'Reilly's poem: "A White Rose", where he says: "A white rose breathes love and is like a dove."

She understood Peter's feelings. He did not send vivid red roses but the deep peaceful love that the rose-tipped white rose conveys.

Colette being a writer was familiar with poets' love and comparison to the beauty of nature. Nature gives so much joy to so many people.

Now the next step was to visit her daughter Ashley and Mark. When they saw both Peter and Colette at their door, it was actually Colette who got the big surprise. She had been so worried about Ashley and how she would receive this news. She thought Ashley might not like to see her father substituted by Peter.

When Peter and Colette entered that evening Ashley looked at her Mom and then at Peter and she knew! She said she would call Mark and left them alone for a few minutes.

"Mark", Ashley said, "come into the living room, Mum and Peter are here" and she whispered: "I think they have great news."

After Mark had greeted them he said: "You both look so good, what have you been up to?"

Looking at Ashley while holding Peter's hand, Colette burst out: "Peter and I are getting married!"

When Ashley and Mark did not seem to be terribly shocked or upset, she said: "Ashley, I hope you don't mind too much."

Ashley and Mark both hugged her and said: "We really had been hoping that you would come to that decision. You are so good for each other!" They congratulated Peter and Colette and toasted their happiness. Later on Colette asked: "How come that you both were not surprised." Ashley answered that Mark had intercepted Peter's loving looks and had told Ashley about this. Again they made it known that they were so happy for Colette and Peter.

Plans had to be discussed and it was decided to move Peter into his newly inherited home first and sell his condo. Then they would move Colette's things into the lovely house in Horse Shoe Bay. When all was organized, they would get married. All this took time.

Peter had been a deacon in the Roman Catholic Church for many years and now he had to make the decision of giving this up, as the Church did not allow married men to be deacons. That was only possible if the first wife agreed with this. But for some unbelievable idea he could not be married again and be a deacon as well. Peter mentioned that he had resigned from that position and he was now free to marry Colette. Finally they organized a simple wedding.

Ashley was all excited about having their sons as ring-bearers. She was looking for little suits for them. At first the little boys didn't want the jacket, but their Mum showed them that their Daddy was going to wear a jacket too and that was a good enough reason for them to follow their Dad's example. The big event was arriving and it was soon time for the little ones to carry the rings. Ashley let them do it a few times. They were very eager; but that was at home. You never know in the church they might change their minds. They would try it anyway. It would make for a good diversion and laugh. So far Robby and Tommy wanted to be ring bearers. They felt so grown up. With only one child it might have been easier, but when one of them had made up his mind, the other one felt he had to agree too. Ashley often thought: "It's always two against one." But she generally reasoned the difficulty out with them.

Peter was working very hard on the move and Colette helped him where she could. She was often sidetracked by her small grandsons. They were so cute and they gave her so much love as well as inspiration for her children's books.

This time the book was going to be about two little ring bearers. Her friend and illustrator, Caroline Bromley agreed whole-heartedly. She saw immediately some cute pictures in her mind.

Peter and Colette went through Colette's apartment to see which pieces of furniture should be moved to the, for them, new house. They decided to take only the antiques that Colette and Andrew had collected, as they would fit nicely with the beautiful furniture already in the house.

Peter only brought his papers, books, clothes, smaller keepsakes and his paintings.

They organized the insulated sunroom as their den and office with two desks and many bookshelves, especially for all of Peter's law books and reference books.

The aunt must have been a great reader. They found books about many different subjects. Colette was quite happy to find volumes about gardening and antiques, as these were her favorite hobbies too. They added their own books and therefore needed more bookshelves, which Peter had made so they matched the existing ones.

All the relaxation books were organized along the walls in the large and comfortable living room. Law books, writer's references and dictionaries were kept in the den. There was a lovely antique tiled fireplace in each of these rooms. The fireplaces had been modernized with electricity. No dusty, dirty ashes in this house!

Ashley and Mark were asked to come to Peter's and Colette's apartments to see if there was anything they could use.

One of the things that came out of the corner of a cupboard was a small violin. Colette had totally forgotten about this. Ashley was so excited when she saw her old small violin, she exclaimed: "Oh Mum, can we have this? Mark still has his small instrument, which he played when he was three years old. The boys will be ready for these violins soon. Tommy can pick out a few bars on the piano already. He really seems to enjoy music and sits beside me when I play and he listens."

Ashley found a few more things to take home.

Finally the moving day came. First Peter transferred his personal belongings and found a place for these in their new house. A few days later it was Colette's turn to move in. It would take them a few days to get everything organized and in place. Then they hired someone to sell the rest of the two apartments' furniture. The condos had been sold already. Peter moved in right away. They had two weeks before the small wedding would take place.

Colette stayed with her daughter until the wedding. It was supposed to be a very small simple wedding, but not only had Ashley and Mark taken care of a lovely lunch celebration at the Country Club, but Colette was so well known in her church for her organ playing and Peter had been a deacon for so long, that many people in the parish knew them well and they all came to the nuptial Mass and the wedding in the church. Mark and Ashley had invited all Peter's and Colette's close friends and all Mark's family came.

After the festivities the not so young couple flew to Hawaii for their honeymoon. Peter had rented a wonderful little bungalow close to the beach. They got to know each other very well during the busy time of moving and organizing their beautiful house. Whatever stress or difference of opinion there was, had been solved easily and they worked around each others' dissimilar ideas.

CHAPTER 16

Colette had been afraid that Andrew's habits would interfere, but as Peter had told her she need not forget about Andrew. After all he had been Peter's best friend too. Peter, who had lived alone for so many years, thought he might be set in his ways and habits, but they seemed to work around each other's different ideas and plans.

To Colette's surprise they enjoyed their honeymoon and each other thoroughly. They went swimming, and sightseeing. They saw lovely architecture, museums, and a palace. There was so much culture and art to be seen, which gave Colette new ideas for her writing. She made copious notes of these new concepts. Nature was so spectacular. Colors seemed to be brighter. It seemed as if flowers and birds wanted to show their sensational coloring to one and all. They discovered a new hobby there just by accident. Sitting on their lanai at their little cabin, enjoying the vibrant view of plants and ocean as background, they noticed a movement in the bushes. Their curiosity took hold and sitting very still, they noticed several birds. Peter looked up their names in the bird book. He started to make a list of these attractive birds and showed it to Colette. She came up with the idea to keep on bird hunting at home. Their new garden had so many trees, bushes and flowers. She thought there would be many birds too. They would explore that hobby further when they got home. They found the view of Mount Diamond so striking. The sight of the surfers was so enticing that Peter wanted to try this out himself. He took lessons and learned the basics of surfing. He loved it but Colette sat on the beach and worried about his safety.

They went to several luaus, where they enjoyed not only the food but also the music and dances. They were particularly interested in the elegant smooth, hula dances with their unique graceful movements of the hands and swaying rhythmic bodies.

Peter was interested in the courts and made several contacts there. He checked the Law School in Honolulu. He had some very interesting meetings with the Dean of the Law school and other Law profs. He told them about his and Andrew's book. They discussed his book, which happened to be for sale at the University book store. The Dean promised to have another look at the book and discuss this with the other members of the faculty.

They flew home after four gloriously relaxing weeks. They had enjoyed their time in Hawaii, but they were ready to start their married life in their beautiful house in Horseshoe Bay.

Ashley, Mark and the twins were at the airport. Not only were the little ones excited to see their grandma and Uncle Peter, but they had to tell them excitedly about all the airplanes they had seen.

Then they all went to Ashley's house, where they had left Peter's car. After coffee and cake Colette and Peter went to their own place. Upon arrival they contemplated their new home with its wonderful view of the harbor, boats, ferries and islands farther away. They made a quick tour of the house and went to bed without unpacking. They were too tired for that. Tomorrow was another day to do just that.

The next weekend Ashley and her little family came over. Colette had brought toys and picture books for the boys and presents for Mark and Ashley and several leis for their neices.

With the boys and their toys they all went into the insulated, warm sunroom. Even the boys got all excited seeing so many boats. Peter kept an eye on the boys and played with them and their new toys, while Colette showed her daughter and Mark the house. They were impressed and they were so happy to see that they had found room for Colette's piano. Ashley played a little tune, which seemed to be a signal for Tommy He came running and wanted to be lifted on Ashley's lap. He told his grandma to listen. He played a couple of bars and grandma clapped her hands. Then he went on and played some more. She was astonished at what he had learned!

Robby in the meantime was playing and building intensively with his uncle Peter who enjoyed himself tremendously. After all these years he now had such a wonderful family.

After a light supper the young family left, while promising to have dinner at Ashley and Mark's place for the whole family next Sunday. Peter and Colette needed a week by themselves to organize the comfortable villa to their liking and to arrange and wrap the presents for their family and friends.

They went to Ashley's place right after church. Their little grandsons had been in church too and behaved! How did Mark and Ashley get that done? They must have discovered something to make them have such good manners. Colette thought we will find out after church.

And indeed Ashley had found two different colorful picture-prayer books about the Mass and the Holy Mary and Jesus. Ashley and Mark each had a child on their lap showing them the pictures and when they had finished they traded with each other. This word trade had now become a key word for the boys. They had learned to exchange or share. Ashley told Colette later that both boys had such a great concentration span. Of course it helped that the priest, saying the Mass had kept his sermon brief and interesting. He was able to convey his message in a very short time. He was aware that grown-ups don't have such a long attention-span either.

The boys were happy with their toys from Hawaii. But

after a while the two little ones showed their surprise! Both boys came in to the room with their small violins.

Colette and Peter thought that they would have to plug their ears.

But lo and behold they played a few bars of: "Happy Birthday." The grandparents could not believe their ears. They were only three years old! Ashley then told them that when Colette had given them Tom's little violin, they had put both violins on the top shelf in the cupboard, as they thought the children were too young to play and the instruments would be safe there.

What a thought!!

One day they had been very naughty and they had to spend "time out" in their room. But being curious and bored and naughty, they decided to climb on their table to see what was up there on the shelf. From there they were able to get the violin cases out. What a surprise for them! They knew enough to recognize a violin case. How did they bring these cases down?? Their little hands worked until they had opened the cases.

Ashley, who did not trust the quietness in the room, peeped around the door, but did not show herself. She could not believe it! On tip-toe she went to Mark's room, she motioned him to come along softly.

The violins were in their small hands and one said to the other: "Like Daddy." Their parents just let them and observed quietly how they put the violin under their chin. They must have noticed that something was missing and indeed they found the bows in the cases. They each tried, but apparently they did not like what they heard. They seemed so disappointed.

The parents thought poor kids they need to learn so much and we better start right now. They were taught how to take care of their precious instruments, these three year old children.

Mark and Ashley promised the boys to fix the instruments but they had to behave. Of course they promised with their angel faces so convincingly. Finally after waiting for a whole week to have the violins and bows repaired, the day came when the twins tried out their instruments.

Tommy had obviously studied his father and mother's handling of their violin very well. He immediately took the manners and stance of Mark and very carefully tried his first stroke. His eyes lit up and he tried some more. Robby needed a little more help but he too succeeded after several strokes.

Ashley and Mark now had some students on their hands. They knew this was going to be a delicate undertaking. As educators and parents they knew that they had to trod carefully and stimulate and foster love for music. Of course these children saw their parents working and heard them talking about music and they tried to copy all their actions They were taught that these violins were not really toys and they had to put their violins to bed (in their cases) after every session, as they had seen their parents do.

Robby loved to play too and he tried very hard, but he needed more help and probably more encouragement and love from his Mum.

Tommy surprised his parents one day. They heard a few bars of the "9th Symphony" by Beethoven or sometimes called: "Song of Love". They could not believe it; they looked around the door and saw their son with a serious dreamy intent face playing and playing again until he was satisfied. His parents applauded him. They now knew they had a true musician on their hands.

He must have heard his parents play it so often as this piece of music by Beethoven, conveyed not only the most beautiful music, but also the philosophy of the poet : Schiller's words: "All men should be brothers.", which certainly was Mark's philosophy as well.

As a matter of fact Mark and Ashley had been discussing

to make this "Ode to Joy" the first few entrance bars their theme or opening piece for the Symphony. Not the whole song, but just the recognizable part. They thought this music so memorable and the concept of "All men will be brothers" could be the basic idea of music in general. And now their little son Tommy had apparently picked that tune as to be so important that it was in his little head and he just had to play it.

At that time Robby was on the floor building and constructing castles and bridges and sometimes he seemed to design these on paper with his crayons, but he often was not totally happy with his designs and would return to his building or playing the violin for a while. He was a child who needed a lot of encouragement and love. And he was not satisfied with imperfections. It had to be just right.

Mark and Ashley decided to play with each child every day. Mark often composed music for his little boys, in which he showed the braying of the donkeys, the peep of a mouse or several mice, meow of the cat. As he said to the children, "This is music especially for your little animal friends."

All this happened while Ashley's Mum was in Hawaii. When Peter and Colette came for dinner, the Maxwell parents were also there; the twins came into the room with their little violins and played a few bars of "Ode to Joy". Then Ashley got the idea to accompany them on the piano and Mark got the hint and picked up his violin and joined them. It was not only the boys that were surprised with their little orchestra.

All the grandparents were just overwhelmed and it stunned them to see how carefully the three year olds packed their beloved instruments in the cases. They thought it necessary to explain to their grandparents: "They need their sleep." Well, whatever works!

Mark and Ashley thought they had a busy life with their music, but now they had another job thrown at them: teaching their children to play the violin and Tommy still wanted to sit on his Mum's lap to play the piano, although they had a chair made high enough for the boys to reach the keys, their feet were dangling. They even had a stool made for their little feet.

The next weekend Colette made dinner for the whole family and the twins brought their violin. They wanted to play for their grandparents, who thoroughly enjoyed listening to the twins.

One would have thought that everything was settled. But, with a creative, artistic family as this was, new ideas kept sprouting.

Colette managed to organize a new children's poem book, each poem illustrated by her friend Caroline Bromley. Their agent sent this off to several publishers. Before too long the book of Children's poems was accepted, but the publisher wanted Colette and Caroline to give readings of their poems and sign the books in several cities in bookstores and libraries in the children's department.

Peter encouraged Colette to do these readings. This was a different experience for her and if it was out of town Peter suggested he would go with her. Then the idea struck him that he had been thinking about a follow up to the book he and Andrew had written. He could do research at the different universities and law courts' libraries in the places where Colette was going to read. He was going to make contacts with the Deans of the Law schools at several places and hopefully find different points of view.

Colette discovered to her surprise that she loved going to the libraries' children's department. She showed the book and the pictures and read a few poems to the children, who were there with grandparents or parents.

Peter picked her up in two hours time. He enjoyed seeing his darling wife so busy with the little ones.

As Peter's wife had died in childbirth, he had never had any children. This was such a pity; he would have been a wonderful father. However now he was a marvelous grandfather and he just loved being grandpa to Robby and Tommy.

Peter and Colette enjoyed working and relaxing in their lovely house. They were still discovering new aspects of this property.

As they now had a new hobby of bird-watching or "birding" they had even more interests in their garden. They observed several hummingbirds attracted to the colorful flowers.

Colette was so enamored with that little bird; she took her notebook from her pocket and started to write a musing.

ODE TO THE HUMMINGBIRD

You beautiful thing!
Did you know that you came just in time?
To cheer up this human must be your aim in life.

You were hanging in there, in front of my window
As if trying to make up your mind
Where to go?

Your aim of cheering completed
You may now enjoy yourself.

Feeding from; the bright blue delphinium,
Decorating my view to its maximum
With cedars as background.

Your long pointed bill probing for nectar
Your droning and humming of your wings
Your dazzling iridescent colors
Give us so much joy and enchantment in life.

Not only here in the North,

I am sure I met you down South
Hovering in and out of the peach, red and yellow hibiscus.

Flowers shaped like a drinking cup
Treated by the Hummer with love and respect
As if drinking from the Chalice.

They kept a book noting all the different birds they had seen.

They had such a splendid view from the many windows of their sunroom, or den, where they spent most of their daytime. The trees around their yard gave plenty of nesting opportunities to quite a few birds. And as they found several bird books in their library, they thought that the aunt must have had birding as a hobby too.

One day they had a real bird surprise! As they had so many shrubs and trees around the house, they thought they would not need to draw the drapes of their bedroom window at night. There was plenty of privacy and they could observe eventually the moon or stars and even dawn lighting up the sky. It never occurred to them that a Peeping Tom would climb a tree beside the window. But one night when Peter passed that window it seemed as if a flash of white flew past. He walked back and noticed this again. He needed to observe this better. The white flash happened to be a snowy-owl sitting on a tree branch. Of course Colette had to see this phenomenon. The owl did not move. Colette immediately thought of a story to write about this beautiful bird. The astonishing part was that the bird peeped in every night that whole summer long.

They bought bird seed suitable for the different birds and Peter made several feeders for the different species. With so many flowers around, the hummingbirds had plenty of food.

As Colette observed the birds flying to and fro to their nests and feeding stations, the writing bug came along and she saw several bird stories developing in front of her.

CHAPTER 17

Close to the end of the school year, Mark was called in to the President's office, who asked him if he was ready for a change? Mark was a little taken aback. He asked what the President had in mind.

"We need a Dean for the Music department and I know you would be good at that; you are young, you have fresh ideas, which is what we need."

Mark answered: "I am honored that you are offering me this position. But I am a bit overwhelmed, as I have so many obligations. You know I direct the Symphony orchestra and have a small family that keeps me occupied and I am teaching here at the U."

He then told Dr. Thornton about his talented twins that took so much of his time. Dr. Thornton advised Mark to think about this and discuss it with his wife. He would like to have Mark on board. They agreed to meet in one week's time.

When Mark came home that night, Ashley saw immediately that there was something going on.

"What's the matter," she said." You are just bubbling over!"

He said: "I'll tell you as soon as we have put the boys to bed." And of course as soon as the twins heard his voice, they yelled "Daddy's home!" A little roughhousing started and there was laughter and talking and showing what they had done that day.

Ashley finished setting the table and getting the meal ready. Afterwards they had the boys play the violins. Not for too long; about fifteen minutes, then another romp or game and off to bed they went to sleep after their bedtime story, which of course had to be a little longer than usual. The boys wanted to hear grandma's poems and stories over and over.

Finally Mark and Ashley were able to sit down and discuss whatever the problem was. And Mark blurted out: "I've been offered the job of Dean of the Music Department." Ashley was happy for him of course, but then came what he had expected: "But what about conducting and rehearsing with the Symphony? Being the Dean will be a full time job, especially the first one or two years. I know there will be changes made."

"I know your head is full of ideas and improvements. That's why the President asked you. He wants more enthusiasm and extension for the Department, which will attract the young people. You'll just have to give up other things like the Symphony. I know you love it, but you can do only so much. And you want to be here for the boys, that's important to you and we need time for each other. We want time for discussions; we never seem to have a lack of something to deliberate."

Mark agreed he would have to give up his position as conductor of the symphony.

"But who will take your place?" Ashley asked.

With a big grin on his face Mark said: "You, of course!"

Ashley was stunned for a moment, and then she exclaimed: "You think I can do that? I am really honored and overwhelmed."

She hugged and kissed him, and then she came back to earth again. Mark would have to tell the Symphony board and the orchestra that he would be leaving. Then the board had to discuss the question of who would follow Mark's footsteps? Mark reminded them that Ashley had been asked a while ago to audition as a conductor for the Seattle Symphony. Ashley was invited to come for a trial performance as conductor for the Vancouver Symphony.

That discussion did not take long as everyone was convinced that Mark's wife Ashley, who had been substituting already many times, would be the best choice. And Dr. Ashley Maxwell accepted the position as official Conductor of the Vancouver Symphony. Mark was asked to substitute or be guest conductor on certain occasions.

Dr. Campbell, the President of UBC was very pleased with Mark's affirmative answer. And he said, "I certainly look forward to the next concert, when Ashley will be conducting."

Mark would have more free time now to spend on his new job, as he spent many hours preparing programs and rehearsing with the orchestra. Now all this would fall into Ashley's hands.

As most of this work was done in the evening when the boys were in bed, Ashley could still enjoy the twins and be with them during the day and take them out. She organized for more help in the house and baby- sitting the boys while they were sleeping.

Ashley found that her helpers Asha and Asita would gladly take turns looking after the boys and would come during the afternoons and prepare meals if Ashley needed to go out or had to get ready for the concert. These two girls loved to help out. They would be making more money, which they needed very much for their studies and they knew they could prepare for their classes while the twins were sleeping.

Mark and Ashley stayed around the house that summer, taking off for an occasional weekend and day trips were planned. They now had some extra time to play with their children.

Mark prepared for the U. fall session and met with his faculty. Ashley asked her Mum to come shopping with her. She needed several dresses for her performances. The men could get away with always wearing a black suit, but Ashley thought a different color long dress or a very dressy pantsuit might brighten up the stage. She asked the female musicians what they thought about wearing colorful dressy gowns. They agreed a hundred per cent to dress up for the concert. They were actually excited about this. Ashley brought this idea to the board. They not only approved, but gave each female musician a one-time clothing allowance.

Her shopping spree resulted in several colorful and stylish, but simple dresses and one black gown which offset her fair complexion and blond hair.

These last few years more female musicians had joined the orchestra. The older musicians gave the steadiness to the orchestra, while the younger players were enthusiastic and ready to try something new. At least that was the notion Ashley had. What a surprise when the senior members of the orchestra were just as inspired by the changes as were the younger generation.

When Ashley suggested dressing more colorfully, the harpist and cellist called out: "Lovely, now we can dress up; it will be more of a celebration."

Ashley was very happy with the result of their first meeting. She asked the members of the orchestra what they thought about having Beethoven's "Ode to Joy" as their signature melody and to play this rather fast upbeat.

They tried it and someone suggested playing the first beats fast and ending more solemnly. Then the concert-master would announce the outline of the performance. Someone suggested playing the Ode as an encore, but this might become monotonous? It could be tried!!

There were several meetings to plan the programs for the winter season. And the rehearsals started. Ashley was very pleased with the enthusiasm of the group and with the results.

Finally the evening of her first concert arrived. All her

family attended. She strode on stage with her fast, energetic stride and immediately the "Ode" was played. The concert was a success and Ashley received lots of flowers, applause and bravos.

All the family and friends met at Ashley's for coffee and dessert. This woke up the boys, who came out of their beds to see what was going on. At first they were a little shy and jumped into their parents' arms, but then they noticed their grandparents and they went there for a cuddle. Colette and *Mrs. Baby Doctor*, their grandmas, brought them back to bed.

Mark was so happy with Ashley's success. The morning papers had good reviews and photos.

Mark found satisfaction in his job as Dean. With several innovations and two new music Professors, he was kept on his toes.

To their astonishment their little ones were becoming even more eager to play their violin than before. They must have enjoyed the tunes they were now playing. Often they would sit in front of their Dad and watch him play. They were just in awe seeing his fingers flying over the snares. Mark loved to show off some of Paganini's' liveliest compositions. This music is so joyful and full of expression, and then he would play Aaron Copeland's melodies which so clearly express the mood of the composer. And the boys would say: "Do it again Daddy!"

Ashley was thinking how lucky they all were to appreciate the harmony in music.

Mark however missed playing with the orchestra. He now played more at home and he was only too happy to substitute as violinist in the orchestra now and then.

He was actually looking forward to the summer session of the Vancouver Festival Orchestra. Even now thinking about it started him off with organizing new programs and what they could do to improve the performance. But he also was thinking of working with the University Orchestra, which Ashley had started when she was teaching there.

Discussing this with Ashley she said: "Let's first look at your timeslot. Do you have any lunch times off or after class times? Talk it over with your staff and get together on this."

Colette and Peter were as happy as they could be in their lovely house. Each was working on their own project and then again they would discuss a difficulty or a snag in their work. They both appreciated the wonderful view from their work area. From most windows of the house they could have a peep over the water or rocks and behold the mountains in the distance. What more could they want?

They had given up the idea of living on Sechelt completely. They could always go there for a few days if they needed a change for inspiration. But for the time being they were totally contented with their house and views, and they would not need a ferry every time.

As with all members in this family creativity, inspiration, the power of moving new ideas around seemed to be an integral part of them. Nature moved them strongly, it instilled feelings and ideas. Their enthusiasm was boundless. Their souls met with eagerness and working power. With two little characters showing love for music and maybe other creative forms who knows what will be created?

AUTOBIOGRAPHY

Born in 1919 gives her at present a high amount of years.

As a child in Holland she pledged to herself to see the world. This promise was fulfilled. Nelly has lived in England, Holland, Indonesia, USA and Australia and visited about 60 countries.

While teaching she and her husband Harry brought up five children of whom they are very proud. All seven in this family obtained degrees from the University of Manitoba and other institutions of Higher Education.

After retirement, winters were spent in Texas as well as many different parts of the world. Last winter Nelly travelled to Tobago and Southern Mexico.

In between time she volunteered at the hospitals and schools in Gimli, Manitoba and Harlingen, Texas.

After the death of her husband she started writing memoirs, which evolved into writing of novels and poetry.

Plans? She hopes to finish her new novel and another book of "Musings".

LaVergne, TN USA
24 January 2010
170998LV00001B/55/P

9 781440 179495